From Time to Time

A Time Travel Romantic Thriller

David Homick

"Live for what today has to offer, not what the past has taken away."

Chapter 1

Zachary Taylor pulled a well-worn MIT sweatshirt over his head. He ran a lazy hand back through his greasy hair and stared at himself in the mirror. Today would be a good day to die.

His phone rang as he laced up his sneakers. Probably a wrong number. After one last look around his apartment, he closed the door and left it all behind.

The first rays of another April sun shimmered across the Charles River as he made his way to his destination. Soon, the dirty little piles of ice that clung to the curbs, remnants of a March Nor'easter, would surrender to the warmth of spring. The season's promise of rebirth and renewal held hope for many, but for Zac Taylor, hope was in short supply.

He stopped in front of a six-foot construction barricade on the Cambridge side of the Longfellow Bridge. His tangled mess of black hair, six inches longer than he'd worn it a year ago, danced in the cool breeze. A pair of John Lennon glasses rode low on his nose, and he pushed them up with an index finger.

With a sudden burst of adrenaline, he put hand over foot and scampered over the orange-and-white-striped barrier, jumping the last three feet to the pavement on the other side. He walked toward the center of the 1767-foot, steel rib, arch bridge that connected Cambridge and Boston over the Charles River.

Zac glanced to the east at the twin spires and cables of the Bunker Hill Memorial Bridge, which had been his first choice in terms of probability of success. He'd done all the calculations, crunched all the numbers. However, he faced logistical challenges. That bridge was always busy and not open to pedestrian traffic. In the end, the Longfellow Bridge had won out because of opportunity. It had been closed to traffic for renovations.

With trembling hands, he pulled up the hood of his sweatshirt and yanked on the strings. He paused for a few deep breaths. His calculations failed to consider the emotional component and the resultant physiological response. Fearing he might hyperventilate and pass out right there on the pavement, he moved on.

The trajectory of his life had changed dramatically the day Harper Gray died. Zac had been working his way through a doctoral dissertation that would have landed him in the physics hall of fame, rubbing proverbial elbows with the likes of Newton, Galileo, Einstein, and Hawking. He'd fallen so far and so fast that the crash left him unable to complete his work.

A man wearing a hard hat exited a construction trailer and stopped to stare. No one should have been there on a Sunday. Zac lowered his head and picked up his pace. He slowed his stride again when the shouts he'd expected didn't come.

For most of his life, at least until he met Harper, he'd been a stranger in a strange land. Studies have shown an inverse relationship between a person's IQ and their level of social skills. While Zac could have been a poster child, Harper had somehow defied the odds. She learned to balance the rigorous demands of advanced academia and the emotional requirements of normal social inter-action, allowing her to travel gracefully between the two worlds.

Except for their love of the physical sciences, the two could not have been more different. She came from privilege, the daughter of a real estate tycoon, and he from adversity, the son of a bus driver. She attended private schools in Chestnut Hill, while he attended public schools in upstate New York. Fate, he believed, had brought them together, the same way it had torn them apart.

None of that mattered now. He quickened his pace again. They would be together soon. He let the thought hang there, and a smile crept across his weary face. His smile disappeared when a police cruiser slowed to a crawl beside him.

Zac didn't wait for the window to open. He took off in a dead run. *Okay, genius. What are you going to do now?* His mind raced faster than his feet. He was smart enough to know that he couldn't outrun the big V-8 engine in the cruiser. In fact, given enough physical data, he could tell you how long it would take and how far they would travel—give or take an inch or two. He considered jumping the curb and vaulting the railing right there, but he wasn't close enough to the middle of the bridge. The drop wasn't far enough, and the current that flowed beneath his feet was not swift enough.

Before he could figure out what to do—even geniuses need time to think—the police cruiser passed him and stopped sideways in his path. The words *Homeland Security* were painted on the door. Two officers jumped from the vehicle, guns drawn.

Seriously? Do they think I'm a terrorist? He couldn't carry enough explosives to take down such a massive structure. Besides, the bridge has been closed for years. Bunker Hill or Charlestown made better targets. He weighed his options and second-guessed not shaving the beard he'd let grow for the past twelve months.

He knew how this looked—a twenty-something, bearded male in a hoodie running on a major piece of infrastructure that was off-limits to the public. Hardly a stretch in a post-9/11 world.

Zac had no choice but to raise his hands in submission.

CHAPTER 2

Professor Myles Gordon poured his first cup of coffee and sat down with the Sunday paper just before his phone rang. The caller ID identified the caller as Silas Gray.

He took a deep breath, held the phone to his ear, and offered a tentative "Hello."

"I hope you're enjoying your Sunday morning."

"As a matter of fact, I am. I just sat down to read the paper and—"

"I don't pay you to read the paper. Especially when your boy Taylor just got picked up by the Cambridge Police."

"What?" Myles set down his cup.

"You heard me."

"I didn't know."

"That's the problem. You're supposed to know."

"It's not like I haven't been trying. When someone like that doesn't want to be found..."

"He's going to need a ride. You better start holding up your end of the deal."

Myles ran a hand back over his receding hairline and closed his eyes. "I'm sorry. I'll get right on it."

"Don't lose him again."

Myles wanted to throw the phone across the room, but his anger with Silas was quickly replaced with new hope. The chances of ever seeing Zac Taylor again had been slim to none. With his return came the opportunity to get out from under Silas Gray's thumb. Losing Zac again was not an option.

What's wrong with this picture? Zachary Elwood Taylor, once the pride of MIT, detained as a suspected terrorist. He sat on a hard cot in the small holding cell at the police station, denied even a phone call. He had no one to call, but that wasn't the point. His right leg bounced on the ball of his foot while he sat and waited. He counted the bars. Again.

Cases such as his required an immediate hearing where a judge, annoyed at being summoned on a Sunday morning, would unceremoniously bang his gavel and send him off to Guantanamo. Floating down the Charles River with a broken neck suddenly didn't sound so bad.

How did he end up here? He'd been destined for greatness. Everyone he met had agreed. Everyone but his father. While his mother accepted his awkwardness and championed his intellectual superiority, his father, an upstate New York bus driver and rabid football fan, wanted his only son to play for Syracuse. One miserable year playing Pee Wee football was easier to forget than the disappointment in his father's eyes.

He earned a full ride to the prestigious Massachusetts Institute of Technology, but it was not on a sports scholarship and definitely not a steppingstone to the NFL, much to his father's chagrin. His mother would have been proud had she been alive to see it.

After what felt like a week, an officer entered the holding area. He stopped a few feet from the cell and studied the prisoner.

Zac remained seated. He read the name Riley on the man's name tag while he waited for him to speak.

"At first, I didn't recognize you," Officer Riley said, "with the beard and all. You're that kid from MIT that I saw on Good Morning America a couple of years back."

Talking about it would only make things worse. It wasn't easy being the smartest person in every room. Technically, it was, but most times it had felt like a curse.

Little Zachary had poured over high school algebra and trigonometry textbooks while his third-grade classmates learned multiplication and division. Teachers indulged him and celebrated his gift like they might someday lay claim to his future greatness. His freakishly superior mental abilities and awkward social skills earned him the nickname Wacky Zacky. Through the eyes of an eight-year-old boy, this was not a compliment.

Being the tall, skinny, geeky kid no one wanted to play with in middle school forced him to suppress the natural need for companionship and social acceptance. These were not his peers, he reasoned. Perhaps if he'd been born with an average amount of intelligence, he'd have been better off. He certainly wouldn't be sitting in a cage.

"That was you, wasn't it?" Riley said.

Zac gave a quick nod.

"I remember it because you were talking about a time machine." He snorted. "I could sure use one of those."

"It wasn't time travel... it was teleportation, and it's only a theory," Zac replied in a flat voice.

"What?"

"You know, like *Beam me up, Scotty*. That kind of thing."

"I'd love one of them souped-up DeLoreans. I'd drive it back to 1998 and convince myself not to get married."

"Time travel is exponentially more complicated."

Riley scratched his chin. "Do you think it's possible? I mean, time travel?"

Zac had enough of this conversation. "Not from in here."

"Oh, yeah." Riley pulled a key from his pocket. "You're free to go."

Zac frowned and tilted his head. "What do you mean?"

"I mean, you don't have to stay here." A broad smile crossed his face. "Unless you want to."

"No." Zac jumped to his feet. "I don't understand. What happened?"

"You got lucky, genius." He unlocked the cell door. "You caught Judge Henderson. Big MIT supporter. I think a couple of his kids went there."

Zac stepped out of the cell feeling like a death-row inmate who'd been pardoned based on new DNA evidence.

"I guess he recognized your name and decided on the phone that it must be a misunderstanding. Said we should let you go."

Unsure how to respond, Zac said nothing.

Riley stopped when they reached the squad room door. "There *is* one condition."

Here it comes, Zac thought.

"Judge says you need a ride home. Probably doesn't want you breaking into any more construction sites on the way."

"I didn't break in."

Riley shook his head. "It shouldn't take a rocket scientist to figure out you caught a break here. You might want to keep your mouth shut and do what the judge said."

Zac wanted to explain that he was a physicist, but he thought better of it. "I don't have anyone to call."

"I figured a celebrity like you would have a boatload of friends."

"A logical assumption, but sadly, not true in my case."

"Then it's lucky for you that your ride is waiting out front."

"What? Someone's here for me?"

"It appears that way."

Officer Riley sat at one of the squad room desks and pointed to an empty chair. Zac signed a few papers as a tall man wearing a fedora watched through thick glasses from a waiting area by the front desk. Zac recognized the face. The man introduced himself to Officer Riley as Doctor Myles Gordon and explained that he'd come to retrieve one Zachary Taylor.

Riley looked at Zac, who nodded in agreement. Zac retrieved his phone and other personal items before being released into Gordon's custody. The two exited police headquarters and stood on the sidewalk.

"I almost didn't recognize you," Myles said. "You look like hell."

For a moment, neither of them said anything. Zac stared at the ground. "Thanks." He shoved his hands in his pockets. "I mean, for coming down here. But how did you know?"

"That's not important. I worry about you, Zac."

"I'm sorry I haven't kept in touch."

"You disappeared without a trace in mid-semester. I was worried. I tried to find you, but..." He let loose a deep breath. "You look like you could use something to eat. Let me buy you breakfast before I take you home."

Zac didn't want to be at home, not today. He accepted the invitation to buy himself some time.

Ten minutes later, they stood in front of The Friendly Toast, a hip retro-kitsch diner in Kendall Square, about five blocks from the police station. Myles held the door open. Zac hesitated. This had been Harper's favorite eatery, and he hadn't been back there since she died. Myles couldn't have known that. Zac took a deep breath and stepped inside.

Myles gave Zac a wary glance as they sat. "Are you going to tell me why we're here?"

Zac stared down at the table and flicked a crumb in front of him, sending it to the floor. "I'd rather not talk about it."

Myles leaned back in his chair. "It's been almost a year since you dropped off the face of the earth. What have you been doing with yourself?"

He'd spent eight months at his uncle's cabin in upstate New York. After returning to Cambridge, he struggled to make ends meet, working in a coffee shop for just above minimum wage, and living in a small apartment near campus. He picked up a tutoring job now and then, but he'd had a hard time focusing on anything but the devastating grief and guilt that he dragged around with him like a cold, gray anchor.

"I've been keeping busy at work."

"Please tell me you're not flipping burgers or pouring coffee someplace." He waited for a response that didn't come. "They found you running on the Longfellow."

"I wasn't running *until* they found me."

"That bridge is closed. You were trespassing." He leaned in. "What were you doing there?"

Their eyes met briefly, but long enough for Zac to see genuine concern. The two had been on a first-name basis, unusual for a

Department Chair and even the best of students. But Myles had been more than a professor and mentor. He'd taken Zac under his wing, like the son Zac knew he'd never had. Myles made repeated attempts, as Zac's friend and doctoral adviser, to persuade him to finish his work.

Their food arrived, and they ate in silence. Zac breathed a sigh of relief, grateful for the reprieve. It didn't last long.

"You can tell me the truth, Zac. You owe me at least that much."

Zac owed him quite a bit, but he couldn't bring himself to say it out loud—the real reason he'd been on that bridge.

"I thought I might go for a swim."

CHAPTER 3

"Jeezus, Zac." Myles glanced around the room, then lowered his voice. "You can't be serious."

Zac shrugged. "Today is the anniversary. One year."

"I don't care." He paused, looking like he wished he'd been a little more sympathetic. It didn't stop him from pressing on. "So what? You think you can join her and everything will be okay? Do you know what a colossal waste of—"

"I don't need a lecture."

"You need a therapist. I can't for the life of me understand how someone with your level of intelligence—"

"It has nothing to do with intelligence."

"Then enlighten me, Zac, because I'm having a little trouble here."

Zac said nothing.

"Let me help. I can set you up with an office on campus, send some tutoring work your way. In the meantime, you could finish your dissertation."

"I don't know..."

"Why not?" Myles leaned in, eyes wide. "The work you've done so far is groundbreaking. You've all but proven things that few have dared to even suggest. You must continue. You'd be doing the world a great disservice if you give up now."

"I don't care about the world."

"I know that's not true."

Zac knew it, too. There'd been a time when he didn't care, a time before he met Harper. Being with her made him a better man. She genuinely cared about the world and everyone in it, whether they walked on two legs or four, and he loved her for it. Her enthusiasm for life was contagious. Ironically, she was gone, and he was here.

Zac's mind traveled back to the day he met the enigmatic Harper Gray.

He'd just returned to Cambridge after spending the summer at his uncle Fred's cabin on Little Sodus Bay in New York, a secluded place where he could get some real work done. The long series of bus rides from Syracuse to Boston to Cambridge left him tired and a bit cranky but glad to start school again in a few days. He stepped off the last bus at Massachusetts Avenue and began the ten-minute walk to his apartment.

Someone called out when he turned down Vassar Street.

"Excuse me."

He paused before he continued, sure that he'd not been the intended target.

"Hey, you with the big red backpack."

He had a big red backpack. He stopped and turned. An attractive woman waved at him from across the street. Assuming a case of mistaken identity, he offered a tentative wave. He didn't know any attractive women, at least not well enough that they might call out to him in the street.

Another man would have spotted this beautiful damsel in distress and run to her rescue. However, Zac didn't see things like other men. He wasn't immune to the urges of a healthy twenty-something male. He just chose to ignore them for vector components, motion formulas, and the like. He focused so intently on a thought or equation that his unstoppable force often met an immovable object such as a wall, or a door, or a park bench.

"Do you know anything about cars?" she asked after he'd crossed the street.

He'd seen beautiful women up close, but he had little experience talking to them. "I know a good joke about them."

The woman tilted her head with a look of mild amusement. "Okay. Lay it on me."

"So... Heisenberg, Schrodinger and Ohm are in a car. They get pulled over. Heisenberg is driving, and the cop asks him—"

"Oh, God. You're a physics major."

"Do you have a problem with that?"

"No." She scrunched up her cute little nose. "It's just that you probably need an IQ north of 150 to even understand the joke." She flashed a wry smile that was somehow modest and conceited at the same time. "I'm only 146."

True, his IQ was above 150, but he didn't care for her tone. "If that's the case, you should be able to solve whatever problem you're having here on your own." He turned to leave. He didn't need this kind of distraction.

"Wait!"

He stopped.

"It appears we got off on the wrong foot." She held out her hand. "My name is Harper Gray."

Zac took it, surprised at how soft and warm it felt. "Zac Taylor."

"Some of my best friends are physicists."

Zac eyed her suspiciously.

Another nose scrunch. "Too soon?"

Zac couldn't help but smile. She wasn't the worst person he'd ever met. But there was something dangerous about her—beautiful *and* smart, with a rather bold sense of humor. It didn't matter. If the past was any indication of the future, he'd never see her again.

A barking noise came from inside her car, and Harper's eyes grew wide. She moved closer to Zac, blocking his view of the back seat. Curious, he leaned to the right for a better view.

"What's that?" he asked.

"You've never seen a dog before?"

"Not like that."

"He just needs some TLC."

"You can't keep him on campus."

"I don't live on campus. And technically, it's not my dog."

Zac raised an eyebrow. "He's in your car."

"I found him on the side of the road."

"And you just had to put him in the backseat of your car?"

"He looked lost and hungry. I couldn't leave him there."

"I could have."

She placed her hands on her hips. "If I were you, I wouldn't go around admitting something like that."

He exhaled sharply. "If I were you, I wouldn't go around picking up strays." Why did he let her get to him that way? He was smarter than that. Smarter than her. Yet here he was...

Myles waved a hand in front of Zac's face. "Are you listening to me?"

Zac, lost in the memory, shook his head and his glasses slid down his nose. He pushed them up with his index finger. "What?"

"I said, whatever you told the police isn't going to work on me."

For a moment, neither of them spoke.

Myles continued, "People like us need to understand everything that happens in the world. We need to feel like we're in control. You didn't ask for this. No one would. But we can't always control the events in our lives. The only thing we can control is how we react to them."

"Everything is under control."

"Clearly, that's not the case," Myles said. "I refuse to stand by and do nothing. I'm going to see that you get some help."

"No. I just want to be left alone." As soon as Zac said it, he knew it was a poor choice of words.

"That's the worst thing you can do."

"What I meant was, I don't need a babysitter, which is what I presume you're suggesting. Probably a shrink to keep an eye on me so I don't hurt myself."

"What's wrong with talking about it with someone who has experience in these matters?"

"Experience? Do you mean someone who's read a few books and passed a few tests? Or do you mean someone who's lost the only person who understood him or made him smile and might have been willing to spend the rest of her life doing both? Huh? Which one are we talking about here?"

Myles said nothing.

"I thought so." Zac stood. "Thanks for breakfast," he grumbled, then marched out the door.

Halfway down the block, someone grabbed Zac's arm and spun him around.

"You can't just walk away now." Myles's voice had a *this-isn't-over-yet* tone.

Their eyes met, and Zac studied him. He recognized concern, and perhaps compassion, behind the anger. But something troubled him, something he hadn't seen before. He pulled his arm away and relaxed the muscles that had tightened in his neck. "So, what do you propose we do now?"

"Come back to campus with me. There's something I want to show you."

A few seconds passed before Zac agreed, relieved that he'd once again avoided a ride back to his apartment.

Chapter 4

Rachel Lockhart set her coffee cup down on the kitchen table in the duplex apartment she'd rented in the Strawberry Hill section of Cambridge. She'd arrived three months ago on a mission, bringing with her approximately six months' living expenses. Fearing her well could run dry before she accomplished her objective, she perused online job sites looking for part-time work.

She tucked a strand of loose hair behind her ear and opened a new browser window on her laptop. Once again, she typed *Zachary Elwood Taylor* into the search engine. The screen filled with the same results she'd seen the last twenty times she searched: a GMA interview from two years ago, various articles from The Cambridge Student, and a handful of mentions in scientific journals she'd never heard of. There had been nothing in the last twelve months. Nothing. The man's been a ghost since the accident. No news. No social media footprint. He'd vanished into thin air.

She held her cup in front of her with both hands and remembered the first time she'd heard his name. She'd visited the home of Silas Gray, inquiring about his daughter. He'd been less than welcoming the first time they met, and downright angry the second.

"I thought I made it clear that this matter is closed."

She was tired of dead ends and taking no for an answer. "Was Harper seeing anyone?"

Silas looked away.

"Was it serious?"

He met her gaze, his eyes narrow. "Zachary Taylor was never going to marry my daughter. If she'd listened to me in the first place, she'd be alive right now, and you wouldn't be... sitting here."

Engaged? "Do you know where I can find him?"

"If I knew, I wouldn't tell you."

"Then I'll just have to look for him myself."

"I can make your life miserable, young lady."

Rachel had no doubt that he could.

"If I see you again or hear that you've contacted anyone my daughter so much as looked at, I will make it my life's mission."

Silas Gray had a reputation as a ruthless businessman. In some circles, the mere mention of his name evoked fear. Watching the muscles in his face tighten as he spat out personal threats took that fear to a whole new level.

"Do I make myself clear?"

"Crystal," she said as she stood. "I'll let myself out."

"You need to go back to wherever it is you came from," he called after her, "and forget about Harper Gray."

Rachel shivered and closed her laptop. The last bit of lukewarm coffee didn't help. Her hand trembled as she set the empty cup in the sink. The tremors happened more frequently amid her unsuccessful attempts to ignore them. Nothing more than a side effect of the medication, she assured herself. The thought offered little consolation.

Sunlight bathed the winter-weary landscape outside her window. She watched the Sunday morning activity in the street below as people made their way to church, or the corner diner for break-fast. A man wearing shorts and flip-flops climbed the stairs of the apartment building across the street with a newspaper under his arm. Technically, it was spring, but the weather app on her phone indicated a brisk forty-six degrees only an hour ago.

Spring had always been her favorite season because of its promise of new life. She had a new life now, and she wanted to learn about the person who had made that possible. She felt a special connec-tion, like the sister she'd always wanted.

Silas Gray threatened her and practically threw her out of his house. For now, she would have to follow the only lead she had. The fiancé.

Myles unlocked a door on the third floor of Maclaurin Building 4 on the MIT campus. The space was large by academic standards, but Doctor Gordon had been the physics department chair for the past eight years. Zac lowered himself into a familiar seat in the corner of the room. The last time he'd sat there, he endured a pointless lecture while his world crumbled around him.

This time, Myles didn't take the seat across from him. He re-trieved a keyring from the top drawer of his desk. "Follow me," he said and walked into the hall.

They stopped in front of a door that read *Doctor Nelson*. Myles pulled the nameplate from the door and slipped it in his pocket. He unlocked the door and ushered Zac inside.

The room contained the usual office furniture, as well as some interesting tech, but the books, papers, supplies, or personal effects that might indicate someone occupied the space were missing.

"Why are we here?"

"This is your new office," Myles said with a small, secret smile.

Zac frowned. "Someone else's name was on the door."

"I haven't had time to requisition a new nameplate."

Zac pointed to an impressive piece of tech in the corner. "Is that mine, too?"

"If you want it." Myles stood next to a 70-inch interactive Smart Board and waved a hand at it like it was a showcase on *The Price is Right*. "Anything you write on it can be saved to the cloud with one touch. No more taking pictures or transcribing. This one just arrived on Friday. It's still a virgin."

This had the makings of an offer he couldn't refuse. "It's very generous, but..."

"No buts. I'll get you a key, and you can move in tomorrow."

"What's the catch?"

"No catch. You can work on your dissertation. I'll even find you a research assistant."

Myles had been a good friend and mentor, but this seemed a little over the top. "The school's okay with all this?"

"I can pretty much do what I want here." He raised an eyebrow. "What do you say?"

This was either a brilliant stroke of luck and just what Zac needed to get his life back on the rails, or he would crash and burn in an emotional and intellectual fireball of epic proportions. While he hoped for the former, he couldn't help fear the latter.

"I guess I'd be a fool if I didn't at least give it a shot."

Myles patted his shoulder. "That's what I wanted to hear."

Chapter 5

Myles had made a generous offer, one that Zac didn't see coming. Ironically, Zac's ill-conceived attempt to end it all had been the very thing that brought this good fortune his way. Myles had always been there for him like a trusted friend. He'd be a fool to pass up such a serendipitous opportunity.

Zac sat in the leather chair behind his new desk, feeling a little guilty that he'd buried his head in the sand for more than a year while Doctor Nelson, whoever he was, probably worked his tail off for an office like this. But hey, this wasn't Zac's call. The department chair gets paid the big bucks to make the tough decisions. If you can ignore the past year, Zac was the brightest star in the department, maybe even the entire institution. That had to count for something.

Zac wished Harper could see him now. He smiled briefly before his expression fell. It wasn't fair that such a young and vibrant human being should have her life snuffed out by some irresponsible jackass who blew a .13 on a breathalyzer and walked away with only a few scratches. Harper's father, the rich and powerful Silas Gray, made sure the maximum sentence had been brought to bear.

Harper inspired Zac to do his best work. So, no more wallowing. He needed to pick himself up, dust himself off, and honor her by being a better man because of her. But not today. He told Myles he needed a couple of days to figure out how this might play out. The whole thing seemed tentative, so he wasn't about to quit his job at the coffee shop. He still had rent to pay.

Rachel sat outside a small Middle Eastern café a few blocks from her apartment on Belmont Street. Spring had sprung, pushing the air temperature into the mid-60s on a sunny Tuesday morning.

Chocolate-hazelnut baklava accompanied her usual sesame caramel latte. The fabulous bakery inside served treats from Turkey, Lebanon, and Greece, and she challenged herself to sample every item on the menu before she returned home to Connecticut.

With a cup in one hand and her iPhone in the other, she perused the latest news headlines until an email notification appeared at the top of her screen. She read it with wide eyes. The physics department at MIT just announced an opening for a part-time research assistant. This couldn't be more perfect, she thought. MIT was ground zero. Both Harper and Zachary had been grad students there.

She needed to know what kind of person Harper had been. Her father had pleaded with her to drop it and get on with her life, but she wouldn't listen. What little she'd found out about Harper had been reassuring, but the well was running dry. Frustrated and feeling foolish, she considered moving back home until she discovered Harper had been engaged when she died.

Harper met her betrothed, Zachary Taylor, at MIT three years ago while he'd been working on his doctorate. The woman appeared intelligent, pursuing a master's degree in microbiology. Rachel tried to picture the two together. She needed to understand. She'd been afraid to let anyone get too close because of her medical condition, but longed for a real relationship with a man instead of having to experience it in books or movies. Living vicariously through her soul sister might be a good place to start.

After Harper's death, he'd disappeared without a trace. Zip. Nada. Nothing. No trail to follow. At least none that she could find.

On her way home, she received another notification. This one stopped her in her tracks. The elusive Zachary Taylor had resurfaced.

The email, sent by Google Alerts, included a link to a mention in the Cambridge Police Blotter. Zachary Elwood Taylor, 25, of 7th Street in East Cambridge, had been detained early Sunday morning for trespassing. The article contained no picture, but it must be him. How many Zachary Elwood Taylors could there be in the Boston area, or the entire Commonwealth of Massachusetts for that matter?

Rachel stopped home to fill out an online employment application, then drove to East Cambridge. Seventh Street was only four blocks long. Going door to door to check names on mailboxes was the best plan she came up with on the twenty-minute drive.

She parked on Gore, figuring the upper block of Seventh would be a good place to start. A small, uninspiring building with four apartments in the middle of the block listed a Z. Taylor as the prize behind door number three.

She jiggled the door handle. Locked. Before she let go, the knob turned and the door opened, nearly pulling her inside. She let out a squeal.

The good news was that she caught her balance and remained on her feet. The bad news had her face to face with a surprised and confused Zachary Taylor. She may not have recognized him from a distance with the long hair and that dreadful beard, but from two-and-a-half feet away, she had little doubt. She'd watched the GMA interview more than a few times. The intense eyes and prominent Greek nose were unmistakable.

"Can I help you?" he asked after an awkward pause.

Unprepared for such a meeting, she wanted to run, jump in her car, and stalk him from a distance. Instead, she shook off the thought and reminded herself why she was there. "I'm sorry." She closed her eyes for a moment, trying to visualize the names on the other mailboxes. "I'm... I'm looking for Amy."

"Oh." He appeared relieved that a crazy woman was not, in fact, looking for him. "I think she's in number four."

"Thank you." She may have bowed somewhat with the words. "So sorry I bothered you."

"No worries." He closed the door.

Rachel, who had peed a little in her pants, walked over to door number four in case Zachary watched her leave. He seemed nice enough. After a few moments, she fled.

CHAPTER 6

Doctor Gordon sat at his desk, shuffling through employment applications for the new assistant job. Zac had been less than enthusiastic about needing any help, but Myles insisted. He needed eyes and ears on the front lines to keep him apprised of new developments and details of Zac's progress. A sense of loyalty and what one might call a penchant for clandestine data gathering was more important for this position than an intimate knowledge of physics.

Three years ago, when Zac had proposed the idea for his dissertation, Myles was skeptical. The idea that quantum teleportation could move bodies over great distances in a matter of seconds by manipulating their energetic vibration seemed like a stretch, but Myles agreed to let him proceed. Zac had worked tirelessly and made significant breakthroughs, even as rumors of a romantic relationship with another graduate student surfaced.

When the relationship ended in a tragedy that Zac blamed on himself, he not only dropped out of the program but seemingly off the face of the earth. Myles searched for him unsuccessfully for several months.

Zac resurfaced six months later with a phone call to his friend and adviser, letting him know he was indeed alive and wouldn't return anytime soon. This put Myles in a bind. His covert extracurricular activities at the Plainridge Park Casino, and other more nefarious gambling venues, had put him in serious financial trouble. He'd planned on Zac Taylor, or more precisely, the huge commercial and military potential of his work, to remedy those problems. But it appeared Zac had lost his edge and become soft. Women will do that to you.

He had no Plan B. That is, until an unlikely benefactor offered to pay off the leg breakers and assume his debt, providing a more reasonable payment plan. Instead of cash payments, Myles agreed to find Zac Taylor and bring him back to Cambridge to complete his work—a win-win proposition.

Myles's cell phone interrupted his thoughts. Speak of the devil...

"Well?" Silas barked at the other end, not waiting for the customary greeting.

"I'm working on it. I set him up here on campus where I can keep an eye on him, and I've given him everything he needs to continue his work. I'm also interviewing for a research assistant who might help speed things along."

"That's better. Hire someone who can get close to him and make sure he stays on task."

"Yes, sir."

Myles narrowed the pool of candidates down to six. He cleared his calendar and asked his secretary to set up interviews for the following day.

Rachel sat in her parked car on Seventh Street, wearing a Red Sox cap and sunglasses. She'd arrived early and found a parking spot a safe distance away from Zac's building that provided a decent view of his front door. She planned to shadow him throughout the day to see where he went and what he did. Eventually, she might work up the nerve to talk to him, get to know him, and maybe understand what Harper had seen in this unlikely partner. At least, that was the plan. However, the debacle on his porch the previous day may have put her plan in jeopardy.

At 8:30, Zac stepped out of his front door and onto the sidewalk. He walked past Rachel's car without a second look. She exhaled once he'd cleared her back bumper. She realized she had a problem as she watched Zac in her rearview mirror. Seventh Street was one-way. She could drive to the end of the block, turn, and double back. But which way? Sixth street was a shorter block than Eighth, so she turned right on Gore, then right on Sixth, but she lost him.

Eventually, she spotted him and followed him to the MIT campus, where she parked and watched him enter Maclaurin Building 4. Rachel considered going inside, but that was too risky. She had no excuse for being there. A second, seemingly random meeting one day later would be impossible to explain away.

Her phone rang, but she didn't recognize the number, so she dropped it back into her purse. Moments later, it pinged to announce a voicemail message. Rachel's eyes widened as she listened to a secretary in the physics department of MIT request her presence for an interview the following day with Doctor Myles Gordon at ten o'clock on the third floor of Maclaurin Building 4.

After preparing a list of insightful answers to probable questions she might face, followed by a restless night's sleep, Rachel once again stood outside Building 4. She didn't know if Zac might be inside when she pulled open the outer door, but at least she had a legitimate reason to be there.

The interview wasn't a total disaster for a candidate with little relevant experience. Doctor Gordon seemed nice enough, sympathetic even. Most of his questions had been off-the-wall, even for an MIT egghead. She put her chances at getting the job somewhere between slim and none.

She roamed the halls after she'd been dismissed, wondering what Zac had been doing there the day before. She'd spoken with the secretary about Zac, who told her that yesterday was the first time she'd seen him in over a year.

Rachel turned a corner, looking for an exit sign. Instead, she found a door with Zac's name on it. She stood in front of his door for a few moments, staring at the shiny new nameplate before she peeked in through one of the glass sidelights.

A laptop sat closed on the desk. She'd give anything for a look at his files and to rifle through his desk drawers. She glanced up and down the hall, then reached for the doorknob. A man entered the far end of the hall and walked her way. She turned and scampered off in the opposite direction.

Rachel took a deep breath of fresh air to calm herself when she reached the first floor and stepped outside. She'd become one of those amateur private eyes she remembered from television, snooping around in other people's business with no training or tactical experience.

The last couple of days provided a huge break in her investigation. She now knew where Zac lived, and most likely where he worked. Tonight, she planned to treat herself to Chinese takeout and decide what to do with this new information.

Chapter 7

This is probably the stupidest thing I've ever done, Rachel thought as she stood around the corner from the back entrance of Maclaurin Building 4 at dusk. If this had been three years ago, her poor heart would have exploded. A few deep breaths helped slow her runaway heart rate. She had nothing to lose after her disappointing interview the day before.

She'd sat in her car in the parking lot and watched a steady stream of people exit the building at the end of the workday. At half-past six, only one light still burned in the window. She took up a position near the door and waited.

Rachel rubbed her hands together to chase away the chill that accompanied the growing darkness. She needed to slip into the building before the door closed behind the last man out for the night. From her position, she no longer had a view of the windows. She'd have to listen for the door.

Someone hit the crash bar, and the door swung open. Rachel's breath caught in her throat when she peeked around the corner and watched a tall man in a fedora step out onto the sidewalk. He spoke in a low voice, causing her to freeze until she realized the man, Doctor Gordon, was singing under his breath. She offered a quick prayer of gratitude when she spotted the earbuds, then ran for the door. A split second before it latched, she caught the handle and slipped inside.

The soft red glow from the exit sign offered little help in navigating the unfamiliar hallway. Rachel pulled her phone from her pocket and tapped the flashlight app. She wandered around, trying to recall her last time in the building. She'd been on an upper floor when she stumbled upon Zachary's office. On the third floor, her surroundings looked more familiar. Two doors down the hall, she found it. The doorknob turned in her hand, and she pushed her way inside.

Her phone lit up most of the room, and she made her way to the desk. She set her phone down and opened the laptop. The darn thing wanted a password. The room suddenly filled with light, and to her horror, Doctor Gordon stood in the open doorway.

Rachel closed the laptop and jumped to her feet like he might not have seen what she was doing.

"Who are you and what are you doing here?" he demanded.

The latter would be harder to explain. She was a little put out that he didn't remember her. They spoke for twenty minutes the day before. So much for her chances of landing the job. Not that it mattered anymore. "It's not what it looks like."

Myles removed his hat and stepped into the room. "Tell me, what do you think this looks like?"

She wouldn't attempt to match wits with an egghead like Doctor Gordon. It was probably a trick question. She blinked her eyes a few times and shook her head. "Wait. Where am I?" She paused for effect. "I must have been sleepwalking."

"Very funny." He pulled his phone from his pocket. "Perhaps we should let the police sort this out."

She panicked. "No. Wait."

"You're trespassing on school property."

"I wouldn't be trespassing if I worked here." She raised her eyebrows and gave a little shrug.

"But you don't."

"But I might."

He frowned for a moment before a spark of recognition flashed in his eyes. He chuckled. "You did indeed interview for a job. We spoke yesterday, didn't we, Miss..."

"Lockhart. Yes, we did."

"So, tell me, Miss Lockhart..." He stared at his hat in his hands, running his finger along the brim before pinching it gently near the top. "Tell me how one goes from breaking into this office to thinking they might obtain employment."

"I didn't know what else to say."

"I see." His eyes drifted for a moment.

Rachel bit down on her lower lip as her heart moved up into her throat. She would have made a run for the door, but he blocked her exit, so she waited for him to speak.

"Come with me." He stepped into the hall and waited for her.

Rachel hesitated before following, and he pointed down the hall. She thought of running in the opposite direction, but he knew her name. They walked to another door, and he produced a key from his pocket. Once inside, he closed the door and motioned to a chair in the corner. He took a seat across from her. "Our conversation in Mr. Taylor's office notwithstanding, you seem like an intelligent woman."

"Thank you... I think."

"I don't know what you were doing in that office, and at the moment, I don't care. I can see that you're the type of person who believes the end justifies the means. Am I right?"

Another trick question? "I guess you can say that."

"Fortunately for both of us, I forgot some papers and returned to retrieve them."

Rachel failed to see how his mistake could in any way be considered fortunate for her.

"Perhaps we can reach a mutually beneficial agreement on how to proceed."

At this point, she would entertain anything non-sexual. "I'm listening."

"I'm willing to leave the police out of this and offer you the job for which you applied."

She didn't see that one coming. "I assume there's some type of quid pro quo."

"An excellent assumption. I can see my assessment of your intelligence was accurate." He moved to the edge of his seat. "I need to know everything Zachary is doing."

Rachel's jaw dropped a bit, and she quickly closed it. "Zachary? As in Zachary Taylor?"

He smiled and nodded. "That's the one."

Okay, maybe there is a silver lining to this cloud. "I don't understand."

"You applied for a research assistant's position. Frankly, you weren't on the shortlist of candidates." His voice had a condescending tone. "However, if you agree to my terms, you'll be working for Mr. Taylor."

Obviously, the good news. She waited for the bad.

"And... you'll be working for me, as well."

There it is.

Chapter 8

Zac removed his apron and tossed it under the counter at Curio Coffee, a small café on Cambridge Street two blocks from his apartment. He'd taken the job a couple of months ago to pay the rent and keep some food in his refrigerator. Some of the regular customers acted like entitled pricks sometimes, but the waffles were considered the best in Cambridge. He needed to stay busy and involved with the world, or risk being sucked into a black hole from which he might never return.

He worked the morning shift to spend afternoons on campus, attempting to resuscitate his academic career. Myles had been right about moving on with his life, but it was easier said than done.

Falling in love was not something he thought would ever happen to him, but when it did, he couldn't imagine life any other way. It distracted him from his academic pursuits from time to time, but not nearly as much as the self-induced atrophy of the past year. He'd been living in the past, a place that no longer existed. The present is where he belonged.

Of course, as soon as you tell your mind not to think about something, that's exactly where it goes. He turned down Sixth

Street toward campus, and she appeared in his mind's eye—the beautiful, unpretentious woman with the lost dog in the backseat of her car.

"It appears we got off on the wrong foot." She held out her hand. "My name is Harper Gray."

Her cinnamon-colored eyes matched the highlights in her hair. Despite the tension that had been building, he smiled. He took her hand. "Zac Taylor."

They talked about school before debating the merits of picking up stray dogs. She pushed his buttons just far enough that it was slightly more endearing than it was irritating.

The breeze that swirled around them carried the smell of lavender mixed with something he couldn't quite put his finger on. Her shampoo? Whatever it was, he liked it. He told her the subject of his dissertation was quantum teleportation, and she wrinkled her nose like she'd just smelled something awful.

"What's that?"

"You know, like *beam me up, Scotty?*"

She raised an eyebrow. "Scotty?"

He frowned. "Lt. Commander Montgomery Scott? Starship Enterprise?"

"Still nothing."

"Star Trek?"

"Oh, that." She made a dismissing motion with her hand. "I'm not that much of a nerd." She met his gaze. "No offense."

"None taken."

"Good. You're kinda cute." She flashed a playful smile. "For a physics major."

Unaccustomed to compliments, backhanded or otherwise, he had no reply.

"Do you want to grab a coffee?" she asked.

He pushed his glasses up the bridge of his nose. "What about the dog?"

"He doesn't drink coffee."

Zac found himself in the middle of Main Street when he let the memory go. A blue Toyota with horn blaring nearly ripped the backpack from his shoulder. Zac scurried to the opposite corner, wondering how he'd made it as far as he did without incident.

He silently cursed that day. Damsel in distress or not, he should have kept on walking.

Zac unzipped his backpack and emptied the contents onto his desk—papers, flash drives, writing instruments, and a handful of day-old treats he'd rescued on their way to the coffee shop's dumpster. After he put everything away, he logged in with the credentials Myles had given him and checked the daily campus news. He stalled, not at all certain where to start or how to pick up the pieces.

When Harper died, life as he knew it had come to a screeching halt. He couldn't return to school. He tried to reach out to Harper's parents, but they turned him away. Her well-to-do father had never approved of their relationship, suggesting to Harper that she take up with someone with more realistic job skills who might provide her with the life he believed she deserved. Zac didn't hang around Cambridge too long before retreating to Uncle Fred's cabin.

He closed the laptop and sat back in his chair, thinking this might have been a bad idea.

Myles knocked on his open door. A young woman with shoulder-length chestnut hair followed him in. "Nice of you to join us today, Zac." He didn't hide the sarcasm in his voice.

Zac eyed the woman suspiciously before fixing his gaze on Myles. "I told you I had to work at the coffee shop in the morning." He didn't need this aggravation. "That was the agreement. If you don't like it, I can leave, and we can forget about the whole thing."

"That won't be necessary. I'm glad you're here."

Zac said nothing.

Myles continued. "I'm going to make your work here easier." He gestured toward the woman. "This is Rachel Lockhart, your new assistant."

"Hello, again," Zac offered.

Rachel swallowed hard.

Myles frowned. "You two know each other?"

They responded simultaneously with different answers.

"Which is it?"

"She showed up on my doorstep the other day, looking for one of my neighbors."

Both men looked at her.

Rachel shifted her weight to her other foot. "Yes. But technically, we've never *met*."

"So how is Amy?"

"You know…" A nervous little laugh slipped past her lips. "Same old Amy."

Zac turned to Myles. "I told you I work alone."

"It can't be easy getting back in the swing of things after everything you've been through. Don't make it harder by being stubborn. Miss Lockhart can help you make up for lost time. You can do all the heavy lifting and let her take care of the mundane things that would slow you down. Research, scheduling, clerical. Send her out for coffee and bagels if you like."

Zac looked her up and down, then grabbed Myles by the arm. He pulled him away for a private sidebar.

"*That's* the assistant?"

"You're welcome."

Zac gave her a sideways glance. "She's—"

"Yours for as long as you need her."

Zac studied him through squinted eyes. He lowered his voice. "I see what you're trying to do here."

"I'm trying to help you, Zac. That's all."

"You're trying to replace Harper." Zac glanced at her again. She smiled and offered a quick little wave. "Where did you find her? Is she a hooker?"

"Look at me, Zac. Do I look like I get a lot of action? If she was a hooker, I'd keep her for myself." He placed his hand on Zac's shoulder. "I want to help you finish your work and get the recognition you deserve."

"She's a distraction." Zac rubbed the back of his neck and sighed. "Can we at least get someone a little less... attractive?"

"You'll get used to it."

"I doubt there are many hookers who know anything about physics." He turned and walked back to Rachel.

She smiled.

"Do you like jokes?"

A puzzled expression appeared on her face. "Sure. Who doesn't?"

Zac took a deep breath. A light scent of lavender derailed his thoughts for a moment.

She waited.

"Heisenberg, Schrodinger and Ohm are in a car. They get pulled over. Heisenberg is driving, and the cop asks him 'Do you know how fast you were going?' 'No, but I know exactly where I am,' Heisenberg replies. The cop says, 'You were doing 55 in a 35.' Heisenberg throws up his hands and shouts, 'Great! Now I'm lost!'

The cop thinks this is suspicious and orders him to pop open the trunk. He checks it out and says, 'Do you know you have a dead cat back here?' 'We do now!' shouts Schrodinger. The cop moves to arrest them. Ohm resists."

After a few seconds, a smile spread across Rachel's face. "That's quite clever."

"Is it? Can you elaborate?"

"Is this a test?"

"I want to hear what you think was so clever."

Rachel glanced at Myles, then back to Zac. "Well... according to the Heisenberg uncertainty principle, you can't simultaneously know both your position and speed precisely. But I don't have to tell *you* that." She smiled. "The police officer telling them their speed makes it impossible for them to know where they are. Looking in the trunk determines the condition of Schrodinger's cat, and resistance is measured in ohms."

"You win, Myles," Zac said and walked to his desk.

Myles flashed a triumphant grin. "Perfect. I'll let you two get started."

Zac shook his head. This had disaster written all over it.

CHAPTER 9

It'll be hard enough to get back into this project without having to babysit someone who probably thinks string theory has something to do with a kitten and a ball of yarn. So, she knew a couple of physicists. Myles must have coached her. I'm not sure how she'll be able to help, he thought. He didn't need any help.

Zac stole a glance at his new assistant sitting in the chair where he'd parked her. He had to admit, she improved the scenery. But that's not what he needed. That's exactly what he didn't need. He needed to find his old notes and other work product. He knew where some of it was—on a hard drive at the bottom of the Charles River. Where was the rest? He had nearly finished building a prototype device that he believed could teleport his physical body to an alternate location. He expected to have a difficult time getting started again if he didn't find his previous work.

"Roxanne."

Rachel stood. "It's Rachel."

"I need you to go down to the basement and look for anything with my name on it. There might be a box or two and something that looks like a computer with the cover removed."

"Sure. Where's the basement?"

"Stop and get a key from Myles's secretary. She'll point you in the right direction."

It was only after she'd been gone a few minutes that Zac remembered where he might have left his work. Unfortunately, it wasn't a place from which he could easily retrieve it.

Rachel thanked Doctor Gordon's secretary, Barbara, for her help and set off on her first assignment. On the way, she wondered if Barbara knew what an underhanded dick her boss was. *I could never work for someone like that,* she thought, then realized that was exactly what she was doing. *Gordon will expect her to go through Zachary's stuff when she finds it.* She didn't like any of this. She didn't even like Zachary Taylor all that much.

So that's the man you planned to marry? God, Harper, what were you thinking?

She unlocked the basement door and walked down one aisle of metal utility shelves and up another. *There's a lot of weird stuff down here,* she thought, *but nothing with Zachary's name.*

She returned to the office empty-handed and braced herself for a reprimand. Instead, Zachary paced the room with his hand on his chin, unaware that she'd returned.

Rachel cleared her throat. "I didn't find anything."

"I know," he replied without looking up. "Do you have a car?"

"Yes."

"I need a ride back to my apartment."

She tilted her head. "Now?"

He grabbed his empty backpack from the floor beside his desk and slung it over one shoulder. "I believe you know the address."

She hesitated, wishing they could both forget their first meeting.

Zac said little during the ten-minute car ride. Rachel stole a glance at him from time to time, wondering about his personality, or apparent lack thereof. Maybe all the scientific equations and intellectual mumbo jumbo that she couldn't begin to understand had taken up the space in his head where normal people kept things like emotions and interpersonal skills. Or maybe he'd had a difficult childhood and locked those things away. Harper had found the key, and Rachel wondered if, given the unusual circumstances, she might do the same.

Zac remained still after the car had come to a stop in front of his apartment.

Rachel turned to him. "Here we are."

He looked out the window, then at Rachel. "Go home and pack an overnight bag and meet me back here in an hour."

"What?"

"We're taking a road trip."

She fired off a couple of rapid blinks. "Where?"

Instead of answering, he stepped out onto the curb. Before he closed the door, he said, "Make sure you have a full tank of gas."

Rachel watched him unlock the door and disappear inside. She couldn't imagine where he was taking her or what they might do there. It's true she wanted to get to know more about the man, but not this much and certainly not this quickly.

Zac tapped his foot on his front porch and checked the time on his phone. It had only been forty minutes since Rachel had dropped him off, but they had a long drive ahead of them. Rachel's car pulled up in front of his apartment fifteen minutes later, and she waved through the window. Zac threw his bag in the back and climbed into the passenger seat without a word.

She pulled away from the curb and stopped at the corner. "Which way?"

"Head for the Mass Pike."

"Would it be too much to ask where we're going?"

He studied her while they rode in silence. She seemed a little nervous, keeping her eyes on the road.

Zac felt something like compassion for this poor girl who had been the target of his unwarranted lack of consideration all morning. Then he asked her to drive off with him to an unknown destination where they'll be spending the night. And she's still here. She's either a kind and trusting person, or she *is* a hooker. He hoped for the former.

She glanced at him and met his gaze. "What?"

"Nothing." He hesitated. "I'm sorry. I've been a little cranky this morning."

"A little?"

"Fair enough."

"Please, Zachary, at least tell me where we're going."

"You can call me Zac. We're going to New York, near Syracuse."

"You're kidding. That's a six-hour drive." Her eyes darted back and forth like she was looking for a place to turn around.

"Yes, it is."

"What's there?"

"A cabin on Little Sodus Bay."

Rachel bit down on her bottom lip, something Harper used to do when she was nervous.

"If you're worried about the gas, I'll have Myles reimburse you."

"At this point, I'm more worried about the sleeping arrangements."

"I assure you. That's the last thing on my mind."

"Really?" She tilted her head. "The last?"

"What I meant was, that's not what this trip is about."

"What is it about?"

"If I tell you, I'll have to kill you."

She spat out a nervous laugh. "Please tell me you're trying to be funny."

"Trying?"

"Ok. It was a little funny... as long as that's the way it was intended."

"I guess you deserve to know. You're going to find out anyway when we get there." He took a deep breath. "I grew up in a small town in upstate New York. My Uncle Fred owns a cabin on Lake Ontario where I spent many a summer vacation. They didn't have any kids of their own, so they enjoyed having me around. It was the only place I felt comfortable being myself. I felt safe."

"It may not be obvious," he continued, "but I didn't have many friends growing up. I was something of a misfit." He offered a wry smile, which Rachel caught and returned without comment. "I loved the time away with Uncle Fred and Aunt Sophie, and I had plenty of time to spend with my textbooks."

"You brought work?" She blew out a breath. "I would have spent my time on a boat or swimming."

"I don't swim," he said flatly.

Rachel had no comment this time.

"After Aunt Sophie died, Uncle Fred stopped going up to the cabin. It held too many memories. He kept the place and let me spend summers there to hide away and get some serious work done. All I needed was my laptop and an Internet connection. Oh, and of course, Fat Frankie's Pizzeria."

"Sounds like a five-star restaurant. I'm sure I didn't bring appropriate attire."

"It's in a little town down the road called Red Creek. It's more of a jeans and sweatshirt kind of place."

"I can hardly wait. But please tell me we're not traveling three hundred miles for a pizza."

"I'm pretty sure I left all my work at the cabin." He looked out the window and sighed. "If it's not there... it might be better if you went home without me."

Their eyes met. "Really?"

"I can probably get a job at Fat Frankie's."

CHAPTER 10

Rachel and Zac traveled west on the New York State Thruway after stopping for a late lunch near Albany. Conversation had flowed better than Rachel imagined, given their awkward beginning. She avoided asking too many personal questions or giving away too much information about herself and her medical condition. She considered revising her first impression of Zac after witnessing fleeting moments of humor and compassion. This man sitting in her passenger seat, the man Harper Gray had agreed to marry, might not be such a bad guy after all.

Rachel hadn't even heard the name Harper Gray until a year ago. Now she spent all her time digging up everything she could find on the woman. She passed herself off as a friend of the family, a reporter, and a private eye, searching for anyone who had ever come in contact with Miss Gray.

Most people in her position wouldn't go to such lengths, but Rachel had always been detail-oriented. She'd never been able to take any situation at face value. She needed to know who, what, where, when, and why; a habit that drove her parents, teachers, and doctors crazy. She felt a strong connection to Harper, and she needed to understand why.

When she pushed him a little too hard about the past year, he became sullen and looked like he might burst into tears.

"I'm sorry for your loss," she offered after a long silence. "I'm sure Harper was a wonderful person." As soon as she said it, she realized her mistake.

"She was." Zac turned. "How do you know about that?"

Rachel panicked. "You told me."

"I'm pretty sure I didn't." He appeared to replay all their conversations in his head. The muscles in his neck and shoulders tensed. "I don't talk about it to anyone."

Brake lights flashed in front of them, and she turned her attention back to the road. She felt his stare as an awkward silence descended upon them. "All right. I lied. I'm sorry, but when Myles hired me, I Googled you. It's nothing anybody wouldn't do to find out about their new boss."

"What else did you find?"

"Well, that you're brilliant, and you had some fascinating theories you attempted to prove, but you had a breakdown after your fiancé died."

"You shouldn't believe everything you read." He took a deep breath and stared out through the windshield. "In their defense, they did get two out of three."

"You mean you're not brilliant?"

Despite the tension, Zac smiled.

They rode in silence for a few miles. She waited, hoping Zac might elaborate, but it didn't look good. She would be more careful next time.

"If I were a betting man, I'd wager you don't know much about physics."

Is he a mind reader, too? Rachel kept her eyes on the road. She thought about lying but said nothing.

"How did you know Heisenberg and Schrodinger?"

She hesitated. "I Googled them... and a few others."

"You do that quite a bit, don't you? Google, I mean."

A few seconds of silence passed. "You didn't really think I was a hooker, did you?"

Zac's mouth fell open, but nothing came out.

"Well?"

"You heard that?"

"I was standing six feet away from you." For the first time since they met, she had the upper hand. "It wasn't a very nice thing to say."

"I'm sorry." Their eyes met briefly, and she saw his sincerity.

"For the record, I am not now, nor have I ever been, a prostitute."

He regained his composure. "Noted."

"How much farther?" she asked, conceding that the subject was closed.

Zac stared out the window as they drove down County Route 16, either lost somewhere in the labyrinths of his oversized brain or simply ignoring her.

"I'm getting hungry," Rachel said.

"We're almost there."

"It's five o'clock."

"I know what time it is." He pointed ahead about fifty feet. "Turn there."

Rachel turned right onto King Road, then left onto West Side Drive, a narrow road that hugged the west side of the bay.

Zac stared out the window as they passed a handful of small cottages. "Stop!"

She stepped hard on the brake, then turned toward him. The look on Zac's face broke her heart. "Are you okay?"

"There." Zac pointed at two walls and a heap of charred rubble that marked the spot where a cabin had once stood. His eyes filled up as he stared at the remaining walls for a full minute before he stepped outside.

Rachel waited in the car, unsure how to proceed. She watched him hang his head in his hands, perched on the edge of a stone fire pit.

This place meant a great deal to him. She couldn't sit in the car any longer.

He looked up as she approached. He'd been crying. "I loved this place. I practically grew up here." He drew the back of his hand across his face just under his nose. "I did some of my best work here."

"I'm sorry." She sat next to him and placed her arm across his shoulders in an awkward attempt to comfort him.

Zac leaned his head against her, and they sat in silence for several minutes. For all her good looks and engaging personality, Rachel's life had been nearly devoid of human touch. She craved it, even from a self-absorbed, condescending egghead like Zac Taylor. She thought about Harper and smiled a secret smile.

Zac stood and interrupted her reverie.

"Where are you going?" She hated to admit it, but she could think of worse things than sitting there with Zac's head on her shoulder. "It's okay to take a little time to grieve."

He looked down at her. "That's all I've been doing for the past year. Whenever I get too close to something, it dies." He paused for a moment before he cleared his throat. "Perhaps you should reconsider your employment status."

He walked toward the ashes.

"It'll be dark soon," she said. "We should come back in the morning."

"No."

"No?" She panicked. "We can't sleep out here."

Zac picked up a stick and started poking around in the ashes.

Rachel stayed behind. She turned up her collar, suddenly cold without the warmth of his body against hers. Zac poked and prodded the pile of black rubble while she watched. He stopped abruptly at the far end of the debris.

"Did you find something?" she called.

He bent down and poked a little more as if she wasn't there.

She stood and walked in his direction.

Zac turned around, balancing a piece of twisted black metal on the end of the stick.

"What is it?"

"My worst nightmare."

CHAPTER 11

The headlights cut a path through the gathering dusk as they drove in silence down Route 104A toward Uncle Fred's house in Weedsport. Zac didn't know what to say, embarrassed by his emotional meltdown in front of his new assistant. She handled it well, and he'd been grateful for her company.

She pulled the car to the curb and shifted into park when they reached the center of town thirty minutes later.

"What are you doing?" It was the first thing he'd said other than his turn-by-turn directions along the way.

"I'm starving."

He glanced out the window at a Chinese restaurant across the street, then pulled out his phone.

"What are you going to do with that?"

He held up his old flip phone. "It's a phone. I use it to make phone calls. You've never seen one before?"

"Not since the turn of the century." She grinned.

"It works for me... if that's okay with you."

She held up her hands and shrugged.

"I'm going to call Uncle Fred."

He stared at the tiny device in his hand. Harper had said the same thing when she'd seen his phone for the first time. He had no need for one of those oversized, overpriced devices everyone carried around. They didn't fit in his pocket, and he could do pretty much everything a smartphone could do in his head.

Harper had bought him an iPhone so they could text. He had to admit, typing on a full keyboard was easier than the T9 system used by the flip phone crowd. After Harper died, he no longer needed it. He went back to the flip when, in a fit of rage, he threw his smartphone into the Charles River. Maybe that's what gave him the idea that he should suffer the same fate.

"I'm going inside now. Any requests?"

Zac shook his head to clear it. "Uncle Fred's house is only a half-mile down the road."

"Perfect. The food will still be hot when we get there." She grabbed her purse.

"I'll be fine with whatever you get." He had bigger problems to solve than what to eat for dinner. In the past, he'd get so wrapped up in his work that he'd forget to eat anything at all. He smiled, grateful for her initiative. Perhaps this Miss Lockhart wouldn't make such a bad assistant after all.

"Suit yourself. I'll be back in ten." She left the car running.

"Get enough for three."

He watched her walk across the street and into the restaurant, then dialed Uncle Fred's number. The phone rang four times before a recording of Aunt Sophie's voice took him back momentarily to happier times. "Hi, Uncle Fred. It's Zac. We're in town and will stop by with dinner in about fifteen minutes. Okay, bye."

He hadn't been able to see it at the time, but he and Uncle Fred had a lot in common, particularly when it came to handling significant loss. After Aunt Sophie died, Uncle Fred lost his will to live. They'd been together for more years than he could count. Uncle Fred stopped doing the things he loved, like fishing and working in his garden. He sold the RV and even dropped out of the Thursday night poker games with the few friends he had left.

After Zac moved into the cabin last year, they'd get together occasionally and commiserate over too many gin and tonics. They'd tell stories until they passed out. In the morning, they'd have coffee. Zac drank it black, while Uncle Fred preferred a shot or two of Bailey's. Uncle Fred had a problem, and everyone knew it. But instead of being there for his uncle and helping him, he poured gasoline on the fire. Eventually, his guilt forced him to take a good, hard look at his own life, and he moved back to Cambridge.

No answer didn't necessarily mean his uncle wasn't home. He could be lying in a drunken stupor in front of the TV. A nightly ritual perhaps. Zac had left him on his own and had been too self-absorbed to check on him after he moved back home.

The car door opened. Rachel climbed in and handed him a large brown paper bag. The bottom felt warm, and it smelled like heaven. His stomach rumbled in response.

"I'm glad you're still here," she said.

"Where would I go?"

"Anywhere without me." She sighed. "I get the feeling you'd rather be alone."

"That's not true. Besides, I haven't driven in a very long time."

"Some things you never forget, kind of like riding a bike or having sex."

He shifted uncomfortably in his seat. "So... so, you feel good now that you've got dinner?"

She smiled. "Peachy."

"Peachy?"

"Yeah, you know... better than good. I feel peachy."

Zac rolled his eyes. "I called my uncle, but the answering machine picked up."

"What are we going to do?"

"Don't worry. I know where he hides the spare key."

"Okay. I'm just the driver."

He hated to admit it, but she'd become more than that. "Take a left at the next light, then a quick right onto South Street."

Five minutes later, they pulled into the driveway of a small white house with green shutters that had seen better days. A light burned in the window. When no one answered the door, Zac handed Rachel the bag and reached up over the door frame to retrieve a key. They stood in the foyer as familiar voices drifted in from the living room. He'd heard the conversation before—Ingrid Bergman calling Humphrey Bogart a coward.

"Uncle Fred?"

No answer.

Zac found him asleep on the couch in the living room, an empty liquor bottle on the end table, and a broken glass on the floor.

Aw, shit. He hoped it hadn't come to this. He should have taken better care of him. In his defense, Uncle Fred wasn't his responsibility. But he still couldn't shake the feeling that he could have done something to help.

He asked Rachel to set the kitchen table for two while he threw a blanket over his uncle and turned off the TV. Uncle Fred's eyes opened when the screen went black.

"Who's there?" he called out in an alcohol-soaked voice.

Rachel turned in the doorway, and Zac glanced her way, a finger across his lips. He knelt on the floor beside the sofa. "It's okay. It's just Zac."

"What are you doin' breakin' into my house again?"

Zac pulled the blanket up. "Shhh. Get some sleep. We'll talk in the morning."

Uncle Fred mumbled something before closing his eyes.

Zac and Rachel ate dinner out of Chinese food containers around an old chrome and Formica table. Zac opened up a little more about the time he'd spent with his aunt and uncle, and Rachel reminisced about a special aunt who'd helped her through some difficult times, about which she didn't elaborate. At one point, she made him laugh out loud, something he hadn't done for quite some time. Rachel motioned toward the living room, and they continued in softer voices.

"What did he mean when he said you broke into his house *again?*"

"I honestly don't know. It's not like I've done this before." Zac shook his head. "He's pretty drunk."

After they'd cleaned up the kitchen, Zac stepped outside to retrieve their bags. He found Rachel picking up glass shards off the living room floor when he returned. He grabbed a broom and finished the job. Uncle Fred never moved.

Rachel followed Zac up the creaky hardwood stairs. He tossed his duffel inside the first room they passed. They stopped in front of a second door farther down the hall, and he held out her bag.

"You're in here."

She took the bag and disappeared inside the room, returning a few moments later. "It's perfect."

"We're going to need to share a bathroom. I hope that's alright."

A playful smile crept across her lips. "Works for me, as long as we both don't have to be in there at the same time."

They stood together in the narrow hall. The temperature climbed.

"What kind of shampoo do you use?"

She frowned. "Why?"

"I smell lavender," he said as he avoided her gaze.

"Oh, that. It's body spray. Lavender and vanilla. You like it?"

He hesitated. "I don't *not* like it."

A small brass sconce bathed the hall in soft yellow light. Their eyes met, and he stared into hers a little too long.

"Uh... the bathroom... the bathroom is at the end of the hall."

It struck him that Miss Lockhart, who knew virtually nothing about physics, was a rather desirable woman.

CHAPTER 12

In the morning, Zac found Uncle Fred and Rachel at the kitchen table having coffee. She wore jeans and a fuzzy red sweater with extra-long sleeves that half-covered her hands while she held her cup in front of her. She did a double-take when he walked in.

"I hope I'm not interrupting anything," Zac said with a sarcastic smile.

"You shaved." Rachel's eyes telegraphed her approval.

Fred looked on, confused, but with a light in his eyes that Zac hadn't seen in years.

"I got tired of it." Zac waved her off like it was nothing. "I see you two have met."

"You can say that." Uncle Fred smiled at Rachel, then turned to Zac. "Imagine my surprise when I put the coffee on this morning and turned around to see an angel standing in my kitchen. Figured I was still asleep, or maybe I died and went to heaven." He held up his cup and flashed an out-of-practice smile. "Unlikely as that may be."

Uncle Fred had been known for a smile and voice reminiscent of Morgan Freeman. He'd married Zac's Aunt Sophie some forty years ago when interracial marriages were frowned upon. However, the two had followed their hearts despite the misguided reproach of others. They'd had thirty-eight wonderful years together before Aunt Sophie lost her battle with cancer four years ago.

"You were asleep last night when we arrived." That was a nice way of putting it.

"You mean when you broke in." His expression fell. "I haven't seen you for God knows how long, then you break into my house twice in one year."

Zac frowned. "I don't know what you're talking about."

"I figured you'd say that. But I know what I saw." He sipped his coffee then set it down. "Last fall, I walked into the house and found you standing in my living room with a big box of somethin' in your hands."

"It wasn't me."

"It sure as hell looked like you."

"Did I say anything?"

"You froze like a deer in headlights." He paused, as if deciding whether to continue. "The strangest thing happened. Before I could ask you what you were doing, you up and disappeared. Vanished into thin air. I never figured out what you made off with in that box."

"How much had you had to drink before you *saw* me?"

"I know what I saw." He nodded defiantly. "I can prove it. The spare key went missing after that. I had to have a new one made."

Zac waved a dismissing hand. "That's crazy." He'd used the key to get in last night, but he'd returned it to its hiding place above the door frame.

"It's no use talking to you. You don't care about me anymore."

"That's not true." Zac's expression fell. "I'm sorry that I haven't been in touch, but I've had my own demons to deal with."

Uncle Fred waved a hand in Rachel's direction. "If you mean your girlfriend, here..." He snorted. "You got a lot to learn about demons."

Rachel held up her hands. "Wait. We're not—"

"She's a... a colleague." He shot an awkward glance at Rachel. "We work together. That's it."

"If I had to work with someone as pretty as Miss Rachel, my Sophie wouldn't like it one bit." He managed another smile. "Probably move all my stuff out to the garage."

Zac didn't care for his uncle flirting with his... his colleague. "We stopped at the cabin."

Fred turned back to Zac, and the light in his eyes went dim again. "What did you do that for?"

"Why didn't you tell me?"

"I tried to call more times than I can count, but you never answered."

"What happened?"

"A bunch of little potheads broke in one night for a party. At least, that's what the police report said." He shook his head slowly. "*Saturday, November 25th*. The second worst night of my life."

"Was anyone hurt?"

"You mean besides me?" Every muscle in his face tightened. "I wouldn't give a rat's ass if every one of them little bastards went up in smoke."

"So, you couldn't save anything?"

"It's not like I knew it was going to happen. By the time I found out, it was too late."

After finding his prototype in the ashes, Zac still held on to a sliver of hope that the box of notes he'd left there might somehow have been spared the same fiery death. "I left a box of papers there."

He got up and poured a half cup of coffee, then topped it off from a bottle of Bailey's. "You're lucky it wasn't a box of cash."

"What do you mean?" Zac said, still standing in the kitchen doorway.

"I mean just what I said." He took a big gulp before he returned to his seat.

Rachel had been watching him and gave Zac a *did-you-see-that?* look.

"So, you're saying you kept cash at the cabin? Why? How much?"

"In hindsight, it wasn't the smartest thing I've ever done. I'd been puttin' a little aside every month to take Sophie on a cruise for our fortieth." His voice cracked, and he paused for a moment. "Guess I didn't need it anyhow."

Rachel put a hand on Fred's shoulder, and he nodded his appreciation.

"I never came across it in all the time I spent there."

"Did you ever go fishin' when you were there?"

"No."

"Neither did Sophie. That's why I hid it in an old tackle box." He walked over to the coffee bar and poured himself another cocktail.

"C'mon, Uncle Fred, you think maybe you've had enough *coffee* this morning?"

"Don't you start with me, young man."

"You have a drinking problem. How much money do you figure you spend on booze every month?"

"You might see it as a problem. I see it as more of a solution."

"I'm serious. You could take some of the money you'd save and fix this place up. It's falling down around you."

"I'm perfectly capable of deciding what to do with my own money."

"I don't think you are."

"Tread lightly, young man, or I'll call in my markers."

"Markers?"

He grabbed his cane from the edge of the table and pointed it at Zac. "You, sir, owe me six hundred dollars."

"What?"

"I had to have all the interior walls of the cabin repainted because of you."

Zac blanched. He'd run out of paper one night while his mind was in overdrive and used a marker and cabin walls to scribble long, complicated equations. When he awoke the next morning, he feared Uncle Fred's wrath. He transcribed as much as he could and stashed it in a box with his other work. After his attempts to return the walls to their original condition failed, he fled back to Cambridge to avoid the inevitable confrontation.

Fred continued his tirade. "I took pictures and mailed them to you, along with a bill from the painters. You never responded."

"You had pictures?"

"Still do. I know you think I'm a stupid old man, but I knew enough not to send you the only copies."

Zac bounced from one foot to the other like the floor had turned to hot lava. "I need to see them. Do you have them here?"

"Where else would I have them?" He shook his head. "They're in the desk in the living room. Top drawer."

Zac made a beeline for the desk. He pawed his way through papers and miscellaneous junk until he found a photo folder from the local drugstore. He opened it and flipped through the stack.

Eureka! Two dozen photos of white walls covered with some of the intellectual property he'd thought had been lost forever.

Uncle Fred's intent hadn't been to read the writing on the walls, so the information was difficult to decipher in some places. But the strips of negatives nestled in the smaller interior pouch would enable him to have the images blown up. It wasn't everything, but hopefully enough to pick up close to where he'd left off.

Before he closed the drawer, he noticed a medical alert bracelet. He picked it up and examined it. "Why aren't you wearing this?"

"What is it?" Fred hobbled into the room, aided by his walking stick, as he called it.

"It looks like one of those medical alert bracelets."

"My sister gave me that damn thing last Christmas. Said she was worried I might fall and not be able to get back up again." He took it in his hand. "Supposed to press this here button to call the police or the medics to come runnin' over here and pick my sorry ass up."

"It's not a bad idea, you know."

"I wore it for a month to shut her up. Then the bills started coming. Those bastards wanted me to pay them forty dollars every month for the privilege of wearing that thing." He shook his head. "Who gives a gift you have to pay for?"

Zac held up the packet of photos. "Can I have these?"

"They're no good to me now."

"I'll find a way to pay the money I owe you."

Fred waved a dismissing hand. "Yeah, sure you will."

CHAPTER 13

Zac stared at himself in his bathroom mirror. He had mixed feelings about his roller coaster trip to New York. The six-hour ride out had its moments, and he'd felt optimistic about the outcome of their journey. The cabin fire was a sucker punch, but Rachel had been there to help him back to his feet.

Having seen Uncle Fred passed out on the couch was another low point, prompting new feelings of guilt for not noticing his problem earlier. The pictures Fred had taken before the fire provided a ray of hope in his growing darkness, the demand for reimbursement notwithstanding.

Something else happened on that trip. He classified the fleeting moment under insignificant and filed it away, but its effects lingered. Something happened in the hallway that night at Uncle Fred's house, something he thought he'd never feel again, something he swore he never wanted to feel again. He'd known from the start that working with Rachel would be trouble, but he found himself faced with a different brand of trouble now.

He rubbed his chin, aware of the unfamiliar feeling of skin and overnight stubble under his fingers. Had shaving his beard in New

York been a knee-jerk reaction to that night? He wouldn't admit it to anyone, not even himself. He pushed his glasses up the bridge of his nose. Perhaps he should try contact lenses.

How had this simple woman knocked him off balance in such a short time? She appeared to have very little in common with Harper other than their interest in him. Was he so hopelessly starved for affection that he could fall for any woman who gave him a second look? He'd like to think not, but the facts painted a different picture. He needed to tap the brakes with this one.

When he arrived at work, Zac found an apple on his desk with a note that read, *you need to eat more fruit*. Rachel looked up from her desk and smiled. Harper used to tell him the same thing.

Zac picked up the apple. "You're in a good mood this morning."

She nodded. "I'm..."

"Peachy?"

An approving smile spread across her face. "I guess I am."

He looked away before he said or did something stupid.

Zac sent Rachel out to have enlargements made from the negatives. In the meantime, he buried himself in his work. He'd been smart enough to back up his previous work, but in a fit of rage and downright stupidity, he'd sent his backup hard drive to a watery grave. Now, he culled his memory banks, scribbling notes and various bits of equations in an attempt to replicate his earlier work. He filled the screen, saved it to the cloud, then activated the print feature to produce a hard copy before he wiped it clean and repeated the process.

He'd never tested the first machine. His theory was that by changing a person's energetic frequency, he could change their location. All matter in the universe is made of energy that vibrates at a certain frequency. Think of water. It's nothing more than a bunch of tiny, energized particles vibrating at a certain speed or frequency. In its normal state, it vibrates at a speed that renders a liquid. Freezing it lowers the frequency, turning it into a solid. If we raise the frequency, we create a gas.

People are much more complex but can be distilled down to a bunch of particles whose energetic frequency determines everything about them, including their thoughts and feelings. None of this is new or revolutionary. However, Zac suggested the existence of a location component within any given frequency. Changing that one component instantly changes a person's location in the cosmos. In theory, astronauts could travel distances that would ordinarily take many lifetimes.

Like the genome project, where the challenge is to identify and target a specific gene in a strand of DNA, he must identify and understand a discreet component of a complex wavelength. Zac believed he had done just that. The papers he lost in the fire contained most of his notes on how a physical location is coded, or what he referred to as location language.

Without his notes, the new device needed a failsafe mechanism. If his calculations were even a little off, he might end up in Siberia or on the surface of Jupiter, with no way to return. Either case would preclude any further experimentation. Just as dangerous was the fact that he planned to manipulate the very foundation of his physical existence. No one had ever modified a person's subatomic structure. He didn't want to think about the potential side effects.

Rachel returned from the photo lab, stopping first at Myles Gordon's office. She braced herself at the door, feeling a little sleazy for betraying Zac's trust. The situation was complicated. If she wanted to stay close to Zac, she'd have to keep Doctor Gordon happy.

"Come in Miss Lockhart. I take it you have some information for me."

She forced a smile and recounted the highlights of their trip before she handed him an envelope containing copies of the photos.

Myles studied them. "May I keep these?" he asked when he finished flipping through the stack.

She nodded. "I made an extra set."

He slipped them into a desk drawer. "I'm not sure what all of this means, but I'm pleased with your work."

That made one of them. "I don't feel comfortable spying on him."

"Don't think of it like that." He folded his hands on his desk. "Zac has had it rough lately. He dropped off the face of the earth after his fiancé died. I didn't see him again until the police found him on the Longfellow Bridge in April. He told me himself that he planned to jump."

Rachel covered her mouth with her hand.

"The work is good for him. I want to make sure he stays on task."

She exhaled. "I didn't know."

"You keep up the good work," he said with a slight nod.

"I'd better get back." She stood and walked toward the door.

"Miss Lockhart?"

She turned.

"Let's just keep what I've told you between us."

CHAPTER 14

Rachel handed Zac the prints. He thanked her and spread them out on the floor to study them. After repositioning them like pieces of a jigsaw puzzle, he numbered each one and gathered them into a stack.

It took another week to reach the point where he'd been when he crashed and burned a year ago. He derived a good deal from the photographs, filling in some of the missing pieces from memory. A few holes still existed, but he had enough to build another prototype transporter.

He spent the next week building the new device in his office. Despite Rachel's rabid curiosity, he kept her in the dark about the true nature of his work, offering complex explanations of random scientific ideas that were way over her head. All she could do was smile and nod. Exploiting her lack of knowledge made him feel like a schmuck, but he still had trust issues.

Rachel was no Harper, but he felt oddly comfortable around her. She had a way of seeing past labels and job descriptions and concentrating on the person underneath the trappings. In her eyes, he wasn't a nerd or a freak. She possessed a refreshing authenticity and a kind heart that was disarming and endearing. Perhaps she was more like Harper than he'd given her credit for.

Zac sat alone in his office with the finished transporter, going over the final checklist before his first experiment. He knew better than to use himself as a guinea pig, but he grew impatient after he'd wasted more than a year. Eventually, common sense and scientific methodology prevailed. He needed a real guinea pig.

A pencil or a piece of fruit would be the prudent choice for his first subject, but the transporter scanned for a heartbeat within a six-foot radius. Inanimate objects would be ignored.

Zac walked down to the lab to procure whatever brand of rodent he might find there. He chose a small, white rat, and dropped him in a cage. He set the cage on his desk and typed some coordinates into the machine. A short trip from his desk to Rachel's. He powered up the transporter.

He'd built a ten-second delay into the launch sequence in case he inadvertently pressed the button and needed to abort the transport. It allowed him time to step outside the radius during his experiments. Zac held his breath, pressed the launch button, and stepped back. Nothing happened. He frowned and scratched his chin as he glanced at Rachel's desk then back to his.

The cage might have interfered with the process. He removed the rat from the cage, cleared a larger spot on his desk, and reset the transporter. He pressed the button and stepped back.

Rachel walked in and stopped just inside the door. "What are you doing?"

"An experiment. Don't move."

He preferred not to include Rachel in his experiment, but he'd lost track of time and couldn't risk stepping back inside the radius to abort. He held his breath. The rat disappeared.

"Zac. What just happened?"

He glanced at Rachel's empty desk. "I don't know."

"What do you mean, you don't know?"

Zac stared at the transporter. "That's why they call it an experiment."

"You made a rat disappear. Where did it go?"

He wiped the beads of sweat that had formed on his brow. "What part of *I don't know* don't you understand?"

"You don't have to take it out on me."

He exhaled. "I'm sorry." Their eyes met. "I've got a lot invested in this, and frankly, I don't understand what happened."

She smiled tightly. "That's better."

Zac held her gaze, then nodded and turned his attention to the transporter.

A few moments passed before Rachel spoke again. "Zac?"

He turned to see her pointing at something on her desk.

"I'm not sure, but that looks like rat droppings."

Zac walked to her desk and examined what she'd found. "That's what they are, but... that's impossible. As soon as the rat disappeared, I checked your desk. That's where he should have gone."

"You sent a rat to my desk?" She shivered. "Thanks a lot."

"He never showed up. I would have seen him."

"Maybe he's somewhere in the office."

"That doesn't explain the droppings."

They searched the room.

Rachel squealed. "Over here." She took a few steps back and pointed. "There. Under the table."

Zac spotted the critter under a small table that held the coffee machine. The rat had found some crumbs from the occasional snack that Zac brought from the coffee shop. He bent down and grabbed it by the tail. He stood and held it up in the air, which prompted another squeal from Rachel, then deposited it in his cage.

Mystery solved. At least that's what he told Rachel. His experiment raised more questions than it answered. Two days of program modifications passed before he was ready to try it again. Another test with the same rat provided similar results. Zac grew impatient. After his subject passed a thorough physical examination, he felt comfortable enough to try it himself. Perhaps he could glean some insight into what went wrong.

His maiden voyage would be to the adjoining office that was connected to his by an interior door. What his destination lacked in excitement was made up for in security. If the transporter failed to return him to his point of departure, he could walk back. After the lackluster results from the previous tests, there was still a chance that it could send him somewhere unexpected, somewhere beyond walking distance, so he added a built-in timer that could be set to initiate his return.

Myles stopped in the hall outside Zac's door and looked in. "Let's grab some lunch. I'm buying."

"Can't right now," Zac replied without looking up.

"We need to meet anyway for a progress update. I thought we could do it over lunch."

Zac turned. "Maybe tomorrow."

"Very well. I'm going to hold you to it."

Zac waved him off, annoyed with the interruption at such a critical juncture. He knocked his water bottle onto the floor when he turned back to his work. He leaned over, grabbed it, and deposited it back on the desk. It took another minute to refocus.

A sound, like something fell, came from the other office. He dismissed it, not wanting to lose focus again as he made the final adjustments. This was it. Go time. He took a deep breath and powered up the transporter, then set the return timer for three minutes. Time check... 11:52.

Within seconds, his ears rang and a sharp pain pierced his temples. He squeezed his eyes shut. A few seconds later, the pain in his head receded, and he opened his eyes. The desk in front of him wasn't his. His stomach rolled. Its contents jumped up his throat and into the basket beside the desk. It didn't dampen his spirit.

Zac wiped his mouth, then stood and glanced around. If he'd been in better shape, he'd have done a backflip or a cartwheel, or whatever one does to celebrate success. He wanted to shout, but he couldn't risk the exposure. This discovery must be kept under wraps. At least for now. He turned the knob on the door that separated the two offices, stopping abruptly after pulling it open a couple of inches.

Something had gone horribly wrong.

CHAPTER 15

Zac closed the door quietly. He needed a moment to process what he'd seen. His head still hurt, and he blamed it for his confusion. He opened the door enough to get another look without exposing himself. The interoffice trip must have scrambled something in his brain, he thought, as he watched himself sitting at his desk working on his transporter. His mind searched for a logical explanation until Myles's voice interrupted. Zac opened the door a little more to see Myles leaning in from the hall.

"Let's grab some lunch. I'm buying."

"Can't right now," the other Zac replied without looking up.

"We need to meet anyway for a progress update. I thought we could do it over lunch."

The other Zac turned. "Maybe tomorrow."

"Very well. I'm going to hold you to it."

The other Zac turned back to his work after Myles left, knocking his water bottle off the edge of the desk.

Zac could think of only one plausible explanation. He couldn't pull his phone from his pocket fast enough. It slipped from his hands and hit the floor. He closed the door quickly and retrieved the phone. 11:51. *But how?* He'd begun his experiment at 11:52, and he'd spent nearly three minutes in the adjacent office.

The pain in his temples returned. He closed his eyes. When he opened them, he was back at his desk looking at the transporter. His phone displayed 11:55. The timer worked. He'd been gone exactly three minutes, leaving four minutes unaccounted for. He'd jumped back in time but couldn't talk about it to anyone until he figured out exactly what had happened.

Rachel returned ten minutes later with a smile on her face. Paranoia took over. Did she know something about his experiment? Did she walk in and see him disappear?

"Why the happy face?"

She shared a piece of office gossip that had nothing to do with his recent voyage. "Can you believe it?"

Zac waved it off. He had no time for such drama. He was on the verge of a monumental discovery; one he hadn't anticipated. It took another week to wrap his head around the results of his experiment and to factor this new information into his calculations. He'd overlooked the fact that, in addition to a *where* component in the frequency, there is also a *when*.

The experiments with the rat made sense now. He'd unwittingly sent it back in time. But how far? Far enough for it to leave droppings on Rachel's desk, then scamper off to the other side of the room. He needed his lost notes. He'd stumbled onto something big that required a better understanding before he broadened the scope of his experiments.

Zac straightened in his chair. Perhaps he could resurrect his old work product from the ashes. But it wouldn't be a resurrection at all. What if he went back in time far enough to snatch his work before it burned and bring it back to the present? His plan would be risky, and he didn't know if he could transport objects, particularly items that large, when he traveled.

His cell phone had accompanied him on his maiden voyage, and he theorized that its vibration was linked with his while it was on his person. Anything he held or was otherwise connected to his body would travel with him. The transporter worked by proximity, so it must go with him to facilitate his return. There must be no space or break in physical continuity for the device to travel with him. Inside the six-foot transport radius, but not in physical contact with the machine, he would travel without it, potentially leaving him stranded in the past.

The spatial component of his first experiment had worked flawlessly, and with some effort, he hoped to understand the temporal component, as well. He scribbled notes on the smartboard, took a step back to study them, then scribbled some more. He did this for the next three days. Rachel collected and categorized the digital copies, then produced the hard copies that Zac studied at night in his apartment.

He pulled off the experiment of the century. Unfortunately, he didn't know exactly how. He hoped to find the answer in the notes he'd left behind. But another jump at this stage in the process would be reckless. His previous jump had taken him back four minutes. This next one would require six months. A deadly catch-22 presented itself. Zac would need to risk an unsafe jump to retrieve the information that might make his travel safer.

Suddenly, an idea blew a hole in his mind—a black hole—that sucked everything else into it. No other thoughts escaped its gravitational pull. It took his breath away like an invisible fist to his chest, and he had to sit. If he could save his work from the cabin fire, why couldn't he save Harper from her untimely demise?

He considered the potential consequences, but they paled in comparison to what he might gain. Without Harper, what did he have to live for? Two weeks ago, he'd been plucked from the edge of extinction by the police. Had they not rolled up when they did, well, he had nothing to lose and everything to gain.

Protocol be damned. Nothing would stop him now. He would jump back six months and retrieve his work. Once he returned and proved he could complete the circuit, he would begin planning Operation Save Harper.

CHAPTER 16

Z ac called in sick the next day. He would have begun his journey from the office, but he couldn't risk someone observing his coming or going.

His nerve endings tingled with anticipation as he unloaded his backpack. He couldn't be sure what to expect when he arrived six months into the past. A jump back that far in time may provide the same result as jumping off the Longfellow Bridge.

Zac performed a preflight checklist like a pilot about to take off. The ten-second delay in the ignition sequence would allow him time to secure the transporter in his backpack and slip his arms through the straps. He made a mental note to design a better solution when he returned. Zac initiated the transport and closed his eyes. The pain returned to his head.

He opened his eyes to find himself standing knee-deep in water ten feet from shore. He saw the lake side of the cabin. Despite his discomfort from standing in Lake Ontario in the middle of October, he breathed a sigh of relief to see the cabin still intact. His head hurt and his stomach rolled from the trip, but the anti-nausea medicine he took before he left kept everything on the inside. The sour feeling wasn't enough to keep him from wading to shore and running up to the front door. He grabbed the spare key from above the door frame and let himself in.

Memories followed him inside, and Zac let them swirl around while he walked from room to room. He wanted to save the cabin from its inevitable destruction, but he'd need tools and supplies. Transportation would be another issue. Even if he boarded the place up and changed the locks, there was no guarantee that someone might still find a way in. He came to save his work product. That would have to be enough.

The walls had been repainted, but he found his box of notes and earlier prototype transporter in the spare bedroom where he'd left them. In a closet at the back of the cabin, he found Uncle Fred's fishing gear, including a small tackle box stuffed with cash. He removed the money and shoved it in his pockets.

Zac paced the living room floor, hatching a brilliant idea. While he may not be able to save the cabin, he might be able to save Uncle Fred. He vowed to call a rehab facility in Syracuse when he returned and arrange for them to pick up his uncle. The money in the tackle box—money that would've been destroyed in the fire—will pay his way. He said goodbye to the cabin and headed for Uncle Fred's house.

An old man wearing a cowboy hat and a week's worth of gray stubble picked up Zac hitchhiking on Route 104A just south of Fair Haven. Zac set everything in the back, slipped off his backpack, and climbed into the cab of the rusted pickup truck.

"Your feet are all wet."

"I'm aware." Wet feet were the least of his problems. Clearly, the transporter needed more work.

The old cowboy turned up the heat that blew on their feet.

Zac nodded. "Thanks."

Thirty minutes and two dry feet later, Zac thanked the driver and stepped out onto Uncle Fred's driveway. He retrieved the spare key from above the front door and crept inside. No sign of Uncle Fred in the cluttered house. Zac set everything down on the sofa, feeling sorry for the old man. The kitchen was in worse shape than the living room. He shook his head, rolled up his sleeves, and washed all the dirty dishes in the sink.

A dull pain snaked its way through the base of his skull while he dried his hands with the thread-bare dish towel. He'd lost track of time. The failsafe timer threatened to send him back to the present without his backpack.

He ran into the living room. The pain increased with each step. In a matter of seconds, the transport would initiate. Inside the six-foot radius, he'd go back without the machine. Outside, well, he wasn't exactly sure what might happen. He wasn't a gambling man. The backpack sat on the sofa beside his rescued work product. He must get a hand on the backpack before...

The pain dropped him to one knee four feet from the sofa. He didn't have time to think. Adrenaline mixed with a self-preservation instinct took over. He dug the toe of his sneaker into the carpet and launched himself through the air. His body fell just short, but his hand grabbed the strap and pulled the backpack down on top of him. A second later, Zac stared at the ceiling of his apartment, clutching his pack like a drowning boy clings to a life preserver.

Zac pushed the backpack off his chest and bolted upright. He sucked in air like he'd been underwater for too long. *Holy shit! I did it.* He took a quick survey of his body parts. All there and intact. He unzipped the pack and checked the transporter inside. Ditto.

The return trip had not gone as planned. He'd lost focus and failed his mission. That wouldn't happen again. On the bright side,

Zachary Elwood Taylor had become the first honest-to-god time traveler.

He allowed himself a moment of gratification and a measure of vindication. He let out a long breath and pulled himself up on wobbly legs.

What would his uncle do when he found the surprise that Zac left behind on the sofa? He might save the box, or he might put it on the curb with the trash. Zac needed to retrieve it before his uncle returned home.

Get in, grab the box, and get out. It would be a quick extraction. He would set the failsafe timer but initiate the return sequence manually once he had secured his target.

A disturbing thought crossed his mind. What would happen if he didn't get the timing right? Is it possible he might run into himself from the previous trip? Can they both occupy the same space in the timeline? He didn't know the answers.

Zac planned to arrive after his previously hurried departure so the box was there, but before Uncle Fred returned home. Pinpoint timing was beyond the scope of his current knowledge. He needed more research before he attempted the extraction.

Ironically, time didn't matter. He could wait a day, a week, or even a month to go back and fix things, as long as he inserted himself at the proper time. But he didn't like loose ends, and he was anxious to move ahead with Operation Save Harper.

He arrived at work early the next day and spent most of his time in front of the smartboard. Rachel asked a lot of questions, and he soon found it difficult to keep her in the dark. He wanted to tell her everything. However, the fact that he'd traveled through time, even if only for a few minutes, required a great deal of discretion.

Zac returned home from work with a plan. He wasted no time preparing to jump back in time to fix his mistake. With the transporter programmed and fingers crossed, he initiated the launch sequence. His head hurt. He closed his eyes. He opened them to find himself in an unfamiliar room. The physical effects of the travel lingered a bit longer than the last time. A quick survey of his surroundings told him that the room was too neat to be his uncle's. Footsteps came from upstairs.

An old woman stared at him from the kitchen table as he made his way to the back of the house. He gave a quick nod and a smile like he hadn't just popped in from the future. Outside, he blew out a breath when he spotted Uncle Fred's house on the other side of a chain-link fence. He ran around to the front of the house and stopped on the porch.

Zac pulled his phone from his pocket and checked the time. He assumed that, because he'd had the phone for the past six years, his account would be active, and the phone would ping the nearest tower for service. The date appeared accurate, so he assumed the time was, as well. He'd arrived a little later than planned, but the house appeared empty.

As he retrieved the spare key from above the door, a police cruised turned the corner and rolled slowly down the street toward him. He unlocked the door, scurried inside, and locked the door behind himself. The cruiser continued down the street as he watched through the blinds.

His box sat on the sofa where he'd left it, and he let out a sigh of relief. An idea delayed him from making a hasty exit with his prize. Zac needed a way to control the transporter remotely and remove the ten-second delay. The medical alert bracelet he'd found on his trip there with Rachel could prove useful as a trigger.

Zac opened the drawer where he'd previously found the bracelet. He rifled through the contents but came up empty. Why would Uncle Fred move it? He didn't use it. A noise outside interrupted his thoughts. He ran to the window and watched his uncle's truck idling in the driveway. Something across the street caught his eye. Pumpkins on the front porch.

The reason he didn't find the bracelet became obvious. It had been a Christmas gift, a Christmas that was still two months away. He berated himself for not thinking of it sooner and wasting precious time.

The garage door rumbled up the rails. He grabbed the backpack and pulled the zipper. It caught halfway. He yanked it again, but it didn't move. The garage door closed, and he panicked. He reached his hand inside the pack and felt around for the switch. Found it. The transporter began the ten-second safety delay. His head throbbed as he counted down the seconds. He heard the key in the lock.

With the pack secured, he picked up the package that he'd come for. The doorknob turned, and the door creaked as it opened. *Five... four...* Uncle Fred stepped inside. Their eyes met.

"Zac?"

CHAPTER 17

Three... two... one. Zac stood in his apartment holding a box of notes and equipment he hoped would erase the tragic accident that had nearly ruined his life. He closed his eyes and saw the surprise in Uncle Fred's eyes again. He wanted to laugh, but the fact that his uncle had seen him gave him pause.

It made sense now. The night he and Rachel visited, Uncle Fred asked what Zac was doing breaking into his house *again*? He'd written it off as the ramblings of a confused, drunken old man. And the part about Zac vanishing into thin air was real, too. Zac couldn't have known at the time. It hadn't happened yet.

He reached into his pocket and felt the spare key from his uncle's house. He squeezed his eyes shut and rubbed his temples.

The box he'd just liberated from his uncle's living room sat on the floor next to him. It had been a seemingly insignificant act, but Zac realized its implications were anything but. Something now existed in the present that had not until he manipulated the past.

Nothing else in the room appeared to have changed. He peered through the blinds in the front window before flipping through the newspaper. He set it back on the coffee table, reasonably sure that everything was in order.

He'd changed the course of history, if only in some small way. Could he do the same with something as physically and emotionally significant as a human life? What about the moral implications of his "playing God?"

He shook his head to clear it. He didn't need any disputes, moral or otherwise, standing in the way of saving his beloved Harper.

Zac returned to work the following day carrying the box of notes and his original prototype under his arm. Rachel's greeting chased the smile from his face. He hadn't thought about how he would explain the sudden appearance of the materials that he'd lost in the cabin fire.

"Uh... you're here early," Zac said as he stashed everything on the floor behind his desk.

"I have a surprise."

A small, furry creature crawled out from under Zac's desk. The animal startled Zac, and he took a step backward. "What is that *thing*?"

"The surprise." Rachel picked up the *thing*.

"How did it get in here?"

"It's a *he*. His name is Charlie." She held the little thing up in Zac's face. "Isn't he cute?"

"He looks like a shrunken Wookie."

"A what?"

"Let me guess. You've never seen *Star Wars*, either."

"No, I haven't," she replied with a bit of indignation. "I found him at the animal shelter."

"What were you doing at—"

"I volunteer there occasionally." She walked back to her desk. "You should try it sometime."

"I wouldn't know what to do." He paused. "My parents didn't allow animals in the house."

"You have my condolences."

"I don't need your—"

"They were going to put him down." Her shoulders drooped.

An awkward silence followed. Zac watched her deposit the little dog in her bottom desk drawer. She reminded him once again of Harper. Charlie stared at Zac with big sad eyes that just cleared the top edge of the drawer. Zac had to look away.

"Well... you can't keep him here."

"He's going to live with me, but..." She turned toward Zac, her eyes as big and sad as the little Wookie's. "I can't leave him alone all day."

"There are rules that must be followed."

"I checked. There's nothing in the employee handbook."

"Then it needs to be revised." He made a mental note to speak to someone about the oversight.

"So, it's settled."

Zac frowned. "Temporarily."

Their eyes met briefly before he looked away. Rachel's heart wasn't the only thing as big as Harper's. She had a stubborn streak to match.

Zac didn't have time for this. He sent Rachel off on an errand, unpacked his things, and disposed of the box. There were some major modifications needed to his time machine, or more precisely, his Temporal Relocation Device. He didn't care for the term *time machine*. In his mind, it belonged in the fanciful realm of the novels and movies that he'd watched in his youth. This mission was serious business. His invention deserved a more appropriate moniker.

He studied his old papers, stopping to make adjustments or jot down some additional notes. Rachel returned and worked quietly at her desk. Zac looked her way from time to time as if drawn to her. Each time, he cursed the distraction and returned to his work with renewed concentration. He pressed on, his frustration growing with each new page. His original calculations, based solely on spatial travel, were far less complicated. His TRD, as he called it for short, needed some serious programming effort to increase its accuracy and reliability. The required updates were admittedly beyond his considerable capabilities.

Zac stood and paced.

Rachel watched. "Can I help?"

If he hadn't been so agitated, he'd have laughed out loud. A condescending glare was all he could muster. His first reaction was to criticize her for thinking that whatever he was working on might benefit from her inferior intellectual skills. However, the sincerity in her eyes stopped him and made him feel like a dick.

For an instant, he saw Harper again. He took a deep breath. "Thank you, but it's something I need to work out on my own."

Rachel sighed and returned to her work.

Truth be told, he wished she could help.

Rachel stared at Charlie, curled up in her desk drawer. Something was wrong. Zachary Taylor had been a flaming asshole when they met, but she thought she'd put out that fire. Their road trip turned out better than imagined. The two of them had even shared *a moment* along the way. While she had no intention of falling for the guy, she thought that understanding how someone else could have fallen for him might offer some insight into the mind and heart of the enigmatic Harper Gray.

Working with intellectual types was no walk in the park. They lived in their own little world, where compassion and basic people skills were not required. Maybe if she gave him some space and didn't take everything so personally, she could stifle the occasional urge to strangle him.

Zac had become preoccupied with a stack of papers that had materialized on his desk. She needed to get a look at them. Their content would most likely mean nothing to her, but her other boss might find it useful. Alone in the office, she stared at Zac's desk and considered taking some quick photos of its contents, but the fear of getting caught kept her in her chair.

At first, spying on Zac had been necessary to avoid arrest and provide an opportunity to get close to him. A win-win situation, she told herself. She continued to write it off as job security, despite how distasteful it had become. Zac's trust meant a great deal, both personally and professionally, which is what made her deception even more despicable.

Rachel scooped Charlie up from the drawer, and the two walked down the hall to a small break room with windows that overlooked the quad. Charlie wagged his tail while he watched the activity outside. Rachel spotted Zac sitting on a bench talking to another man. She strained to get a look at the unfamiliar face, but decided that his identity could wait. She rushed back to the office to sell her soul again in the name of job security.

With Charlie back in his drawer, she began snapping photos of the papers on Zac's desk. She had no idea how long his conversation might last, but he would need a full five minutes to walk back to the office from his present location. She kept an eye on the clock while she worked.

Zac returned well after she'd finished. He gathered everything off his desk and deposited it in a leather case. Neither spoke before he left the office.

Zac walked home, dropped his things at the door, and headed for the kitchen to find some aspirin. He'd had more than his share of headaches lately, but he wasn't ready to blame it on his relocation activity. The antique brass kettle that he put on the stove had belonged to Harper, one of the few things he took from her apartment after she died. She loved her tea and sampled all the latest exotic blends. He'd humored her at first, but soon grew to love the time they shared chatting over a steaming cup.

Gotu Kola tea is known to reduce anxiety and depression. It had been Zac's drink of choice during that difficult first year. While it appeared he might need some help again in those areas, the tea's ability to boost cognitive function was what he was after today.

The TRD required more work. The fact that he would be hurling himself through time instead of some nameless rodent would justify upgrading some components. None of that would matter if he didn't get the program fixed. Zac admitted he needed help—help that cost money he didn't have. He needed to find an angel investor.

The logical first step would be to ask Myles for money, but that would require a reason for needing the additional funding. He couldn't tell Myles what he was doing or why he was doing it. Making up some bullshit story to cover his tracks was not an option. Myles would see through the attempted subterfuge.

Earlier that day, Zac met with an old friend from the IT department, hoping for some pro bono assistance with programming the TRD. Unfortunately, his friend was unable to help. Zac's remaining options involved contracting out the work, which brought him back to his lack of funds.

Zac had an idea so bold that he dismissed it at first, but extraordinary times call for extraordinary measures. The plan was risky, requiring him to divulge his secret and place his life in the hands of someone he didn't trust. It required a meeting with Silas Gray.

CHAPTER 18

Myles beamed with satisfaction as he watched Rachel leave his office, pleased that their little arrangement had proceeded as planned. He wore a twisted smile as he examined the new photos Rachel had provided. After an hour of intense scrutiny, he removed his glasses, sat back in his chair, and rubbed his temples. Something was wrong. Zac had gone off the rails, heading in a different direction. That may be why he'd become increasingly guarded in their weekly status meetings.

He'd always thought of Zac as something of a savant, so he assumed that wherever this project was now headed, it could have far-reaching economic, as well as scientific, implications. Unfortunately, much of Zac's calculations were beyond his area of expertise.

After some deliberation, Myles picked up the phone. He needed someone to help him make sense of Zac's work. He dialed a few numbers, then stopped and set the phone down. This information is best kept to himself for the time being. He might have to explain how he came to possess the photos and why he wouldn't simply ask Zac for an explanation. The answers to those questions were something he'd rather not share.

Myles needed to lean on Miss Lockhart for more information. The equations and other work product she'd provided meant little to him without help to decipher their exact meaning. They required context. His informant needed to step up her game and get close enough to Zac that he might confide in her more freely about what he was working on. If he played his cards right, he might turn Zac's work into a personal payday.

An audience with the Pope would be easier to arrange than a meeting with Silas Gray, but Zac's entire project now depended on it. Numerous attempts to reach the man at his office had fallen short, so Zac paid him a visit at his home on Saturday. He planned to wedge his foot inside the door like a determined salesman. Walking along the 10-foot-high, wrought-iron fence that surrounded Silas Gray's mansion, he realized that wasn't going to happen. He stabbed the intercom button when he reached the massive gate.

A metallic voice informed Zac that Mr. Gray was unavailable. Zac didn't buy it. He assured the palace guard that he, in fact, knew Mr. Gray very well, and needed to speak with him. The voice from inside the tiny speaker instructed him to wait. Zac's stomach did a lazy barrel roll. Silas hated his guts. He blamed him for his daughter's death.

Silas was not the only one who blamed him for the accident. Harper wouldn't have stormed out of the apartment and drove off if they hadn't had that stupid argument. He'd been dragging that guilt around with him like a bag of rocks. If Silas agreed to see him, it would most likely be to lock him up somewhere in the bowels of his castle and throw away the key. Perhaps it's what he deserved. Regardless, Zac needed to take the chance.

The speaker crackled, and the voice returned. "Mr. Gray is still unavailable. The police, however, are on the way as we speak. You should go now and never come back."

Zac, who'd never been in a fight in his life, squeezed his hands into fists at the snarky remark.

"Listen, you little shit. You tell him if he ever wants to see his daughter again, he'll hear me out." The words came out before Zac had time to think.

"Tick-tock, Mr. Taylor."

A siren wailed in the distance. Plan B had failed. He didn't have a Plan C. Yet. Another run-in with the law was not something he wanted to deal with.

Zac's hands tightened into fists as he marched toward campus. He'd half-expected Silas to be unavailable or otherwise refuse to see him. It represented a setback, nonetheless. He had no backup plan, no alternative funding sources. He shook it off and focused on the changes to the TRD that didn't require high-level programming. A remote control would eliminate another potential debacle like the one he'd had at Uncle Fred's.

Rachel looked up from Zac's desk when he opened the office door, her hand in the proverbial cookie jar.

CHAPTER 19

Zac didn't know what to say. Rachel remained silent. They stared at each other for what felt like five minutes. Zac spoke first.

"What are you doing here?"

"I... I..."

"Did you forget which desk was yours?" When she didn't respond, he pointed to her desk in the corner. "I'm pretty sure that's yours over there."

She closed his laptop and stood. "Zac, I'm so sorry, I..."

"Don't talk."

Zac hated confrontation. He avoided it whenever possible. "Just leave. I have work to do, and I don't think I can do it with you here."

"I don't know what I was thinking. It won't happen again."

He avoided her eyes. "You need to take some time off while I sort things out."

"How much time?" She wrung her hands while her eyes pleaded for mercy.

"I'll let you know."

Zac watched, disappointed, as she slunk out of the office. Why would she do that? He'd be more careful if and when he let her back. In the meantime, he had work to do.

Uncle Fred's medical alert bracelet had given him the idea of a remote control for the TRD. However, that transmitter uses the cellular network to connect with the dispatch office. Impractical for such a short distance and unreliable for his application. Next, he considered a television remote, but because they use infrared, line-of-sight transmission, it would be unworkable, as well.

The memory of his ill-fated trip to his uncle's house resurfaced. Annoyed, he tried unsuccessfully to shake it off. He recalled watching his uncle's truck idling in the driveway while the garage door rumbled up the rails. That's it, he thought. A garage door remote is a radio transmitter that sends a signal to a built-in radio receiver on the opener.

Where was his assistant when he needed her? He almost laughed. It wasn't funny. He blamed Myles. Zac never asked for an assistant. He'd always worked alone. Somehow, he'd developed feelings for this woman, and that was unacceptable. He wasn't sure who to blame for that.

Zac fought the Saturday crowd at the mall. The salesman at Home Depot wasted time asking about the size of the door and a hundred other questions. Zac told him he didn't have a garage. He added that he planned to take the thing apart, remove the remote transceiver, and install it in his time machine. The salesman couldn't get him out of the store fast enough.

He returned to campus, unpacked his new garage door opener, and studied the part of the instruction manual that most people ignore—the electrical schematic in the back. He located a screwdriver, removed the receiver, and installed it in the TRD. The transmitter was smaller than he'd imagined, and he debated strapping it to his wrist or carrying it in his pocket. Ultimately, the wrist idea won out.

Zac didn't want to wait for the program modifications, which might take weeks. He needed to test his upgraded TRD now. He wasn't himself lately, sidestepping protocol and taking unnecessary chances, but he'd grown impatient to rescue Harper and get on with his life. A quick trip—an hour into the past—to his current location would allow him to test the remote feature with little risk. If the new feature didn't work, he'd still be in his office, but with an extra hour to fix it.

He set the coordinates, threw his backpack over his shoulder, and pressed the button on the wrist transmitter. Immediately, his head throbbed and an invisible fist punched his stomach. He closed his eyes and opened them again to find himself sitting in the second-floor lounge. He looked around to see if anyone had noticed his sudden appearance.

Several people went about their business as if nothing had happened, suggesting that he had arrived undetected. That was the good news. The bad news was that no one should have been there on a Saturday.

His suspicions were confirmed when he checked his phone. Not only did he not land in his office as planned, he did not land on Saturday. Instead of traveling an hour into the past, he'd traveled a full day. The TRD needed more work before he would consider a trip back to last year.

Zac had set the failsafe for one hour, and he was in no hurry to get back. He wondered what might happen if he manually disabled the failsafe and didn't go back at all, reliving the previous day. He poured himself a cup of coffee and returned to his seat. An interesting experiment, he thought. What might he do differently this time, and what effect would it have on the rest of the timeline?

Friday had been an uneventful day, except for the old woman he met on his way home who had stepped into the street at the corner of Main and Vassar. Zac pulled her from the path of a turning car that would have hit her. What if he wasn't so gallant this time? Could he do that? She would be struck, perhaps even killed. The timeline would surely be affected. Maybe not for him, but for the woman, the driver, her family, his family, the first responders. The list goes on. Like throwing a stone into a still pond, the ripples would spread. There's no way to tell how far.

Because of his heroic actions the day before, the woman went safely on her way. We know that. It's a fact. If he traveled back now and withheld his assistance, he would intentionally cause her harm, or even death. Such moral gray areas might only be the tip of the iceberg. In Harper's case, his actions would save a life rather than take one. How could that be a bad thing?

He crushed his styrofoam cup and deposited it in the basket on his way out the door. His trip hadn't been a total bust. The remote control worked like a charm. However, he thought it best not to attempt any more trips until after the programming updates.

Zac passed Myles's door on the way to his office. Heated words escaped from inside. The conversation seemed one-sided, and Zac wondered who was suffering the wrath of Myles Gordon this time. Someone had failed an assignment, putting their job in jeopardy if they didn't step up their game.

Zac walked past the empty secretary's desk to catch a glimpse through the crack in the door. Before he got a look at the poor soul, Myles mentioned Zac's name. Zac froze. He closed his eyes and listened.

"I need details," Myles bellowed. "What you've given me so far isn't enough."

A woman cried.

"If Zachary Taylor so much as blows his nose, I want to know about it. I need to know everything that he's working on, and you're going to tell me, or else."

Zac frowned. His heart pumped harder. He wanted to know who was on the other end of the conversation. When he moved closer to get a better look, his heart stopped.

CHAPTER 20

Zac pressed the button on his wrist and returned to his office. Satisfied that the return trip went off without a hitch, he rummaged through Rachel's drawers, looking for evidence of her betrayal. He wouldn't have believed it if he hadn't heard it with his own ears and seen it with his own eyes.

His investigation turned up nothing but a broken heart. He leaned back in her chair and felt sorry for her as his initial anger dissipated. Myles had bullied her into spying on him, maybe even blackmailed her with employment. Why else would he hire an assistant who knew nothing about physics?

How could he have fallen for Myles's phony concern? His betrayal hurt more than Rachel's. Zac hadn't known Rachel all that long. Myles had been like a father to him for the past four years. When his biological father had expressed only disappointment, Myles had believed in him and took him under his wing. Now, it appeared he had ulterior motives.

Zac's phone rang. An unfamiliar number. He opened it but said nothing.

"What did you mean, *if I ever want to see her again?*"

Zac nearly dropped the phone. "How... how did you get this number?"

"I'm a powerful man, Mr. Taylor."

"Zac."

"I'll ask you one more time, Mr. Taylor. What did you mean?"

"I think we can help each other."

"I'm listening."

"Can we meet?"

"Why don't we just get this over with right now."

"Because I don't trust the phone. What I have to say is for your ears only."

"Very well." Silas Gray coughed a wet cough, probably the result of smoking big fat cigars for most of his adult life. "Where are you now?"

"School."

"I'll pick you up in front of the auditorium in thirty minutes."

The line went dead.

Zac had a foot in the door, an audience with the Pope. He slipped his backpack over his shoulder, no longer able to trust anyone. The walk to Kresge Auditorium took only ten minutes. Zac sat on the steps thinking about how much to tell Silas. Who was he kidding? His back was up against the wall. He would tell him whatever was necessary to get the money he needed to continue his project.

Fifteen minutes later, a long, black limo slid into the pull-off on the Amherst Street side of the auditorium. Zac's heart raced as he flagged it down. He climbed into the large back seat, and the car pulled away.

Silas pressed a button on the armrest and an electric motor whirred. Zac watched a wall of Plexiglass rise from the seatback in front of them. It stopped at the roof with a click. Sealed inside a soundproof bubble, Silas spoke.

"I wish I could say that it was good to see you again."

While it wasn't an accusation, the taste of guilt and shame climbed up the back of his throat.

"I don't have a lot of time, so you'd better get to the point."

Asking for money to build a time machine might be a hard sell. He had to pull out all the stops. He started with a condensed version of his theory and experimentation to date, then described his plan to travel back in time and prevent the accident that killed Silas's daughter.

Silas stared out the window without speaking.

Zac held his breath. His future depended on what this powerful man might say next.

"I'm not sure what I expected to hear today," he said without moving, "but this certainly wasn't it."

Silas turned to Zac and continued. "Harper insisted that the boy she met at school was a genius. That's the word she used: genius. Of course, I didn't share her views on many things." Silas paused. "I'm sure it's no secret that I never liked you."

Zac swallowed hard.

Silas studied him through squinted eyes before he continued. "Now, I don't know whether you're a genius or a lunatic."

It appeared he had a 50-50 chance. "I can do this. It's just that I've run out of funds to complete the refinements I need to ensure the equipment works properly."

"And in exchange for my money, Harper lives?"

"Yes. That would be the deal."

He turned to the window again. "Harper and I had a complicated relationship. Like oil and water, we never mixed. We had a falling out, and I regret that we didn't have time to reconcile before her untimely death."

"I'm sorry for your loss, sir, and I—"

"If you're trying to pull a fast one, playing on the emotions of a grieving father..." He turned to Zac and spoke matter-of-factly. "I will destroy you."

Silas didn't make idle threats. A thousand spiders crawled up Zac's arms and down his back. "I have as much at stake here as you."

Silas glared. "How much is this going to cost me?"

Zac had already secured estimates from a few programmers who had come highly recommended. With a check from Silas, he could hit the ground running.

"Sixty thousand should cover my expenses. I will gladly return any unused funds."

The look on Silas's face led Zac to believe he expected the bill to be much higher.

"If I give you the money, and that's a big if, what proof do I have that you'll hold up your end of the deal?"

"Well... I..." Zac hadn't considered that Silas might want assurance that he could do what he promised. "What kind of proof do you need?"

"You've got to admit that your idea is a little far-fetched. I might as well be financing a science-fiction movie script. You need to at least prove to me that this time machine of yours works. A proof of concept, so to speak."

"The machine needs more work. That's why I need the money."

"No proof. No money."

The collar of Zac's shirt shrunk, and he hooked a finger inside to tug at it. Another trip at this point would be dangerous, but it appeared he didn't have a choice.

"Tell me how I can prove it to you."

Silas rubbed his chin while he stared out the window. Several minutes passed before he spoke again.

"When Harper passed, I cursed her for leaving. I know it wasn't her fault, but it felt like she did it to hurt me. One night, I got drunk and terribly upset. I destroyed many things in my house that night. One, I regret more than the others."

"What was it?"

"A picture I had taken with Harper on Christmas many years ago. She had a light in her eyes and the world at her feet. She grew up after that and turned on me, but sometimes after we'd fought, I'd look at that picture and pretend she was still my little girl."

Zac hesitated, waiting for him to add something more.

Silas turned. "I want you to bring that photo back to me."

CHAPTER 21

Zac watched the limo drive away, a little less enthusiastic than when it had arrived. He'd have to make another trip back before the necessary programming modifications. He couldn't fault Silas for wanting proof. After all, what Zac had proposed was a little out of the ordinary, to put it mildly.

Silas had promised to email the floor plans for the house. His target would be on a shelf in a second-floor office. Fortunately, the house was large enough that, even if his calculations were off as much as when he visited Uncle Fred's, he'd still land somewhere inside. If not, getting past the guards would be a problem.

Zac paced inside his office, waiting for that email. He wanted to put this trip behind him and move on. He'd asked Silas to identify a time before he destroyed the picture that he would not be home. Zac didn't want to risk running into him in his travels.

A ping from his laptop signaled an incoming email. Zac opened it and downloaded the floor plans. He printed them, then determined the coordinates for Silas's office. He programmed the date, time, and location into the TRD and loaded it into his backpack. With Rachel sidelined, he locked the door and planned to leave from the office. He fastened the remote to his wrist, pressed the button, and disappeared into the past.

Zac opened his eyes and shook the residual pain from his head. He stood in a large pantry. After the trip to Uncle Fred's, he'd purchased a hand-held GPS unit. The coordinates didn't match. He leaned his head back, his eyes drawn to the design of the tin ceiling. It occurred to him that GPS coordinates are dots on a map with no allowance for elevation.

He pulled out the printed floor plans and located a pantry adjacent to the kitchen on the ground floor. His target was one floor up and three rooms to the east. Close enough for this trip, but something that needed to be fixed. He wasn't sure if he could build the elevation component into his equation, but it would be a useful bit of information. Landing inside a walk-in freezer or a large trash compactor one or two floors directly above or below his target could prove disastrous.

A noise came from somewhere in the kitchen. He couldn't just walk out of the pantry and expect to be allowed to stroll through the house. The plans showed a commercial dumbwaiter in a location that appeared to be a solid wall of cabinets. Zac opened one, then another. He found his prize behind door number three.

The dumbwaiter appeared just large enough for him to crawl inside. Unpleasant memories of being stuffed inside a middle-school gym locker surfaced. He shook them off. The controls looked like they'd been updated within the last twenty years, so he climbed aboard, pressed the up button, and pulled the access door closed. He would have preferred a traditional elevator, but he had a job to do.

The motor worked smoothly and quietly and stopped with a jolt on the second floor. Zac pushed the door open a crack to survey what appeared to be a private drawing room. He unfolded himself onto the thick carpet and stretched out the kinks. Footsteps in the hall forced him to scramble for cover behind a large wingback chair. The hallway door opened, and a young woman in a uniform carrying a large plastic bag entered the room. She walked directly to an ornately carved end table beside an oversized leather recliner.

Zac nearly gasped when he realized he hadn't closed the dumbwaiter door. He covered his mouth and turned back toward the woman. She emptied an ashtray into the bag, picked up a brandy snifter, and left the room. Zac exhaled, grateful for her laser-like focus, or maybe her indifference. He waited a few minutes while he checked the floor plan, then walked to the door.

A glance outside revealed no activity in the hall. He crept to the third door on the right and peeked inside. Silas had assured him he'd been out of town on this particular day, so he walked in and gently closed the door behind himself.

Zac paused, intimidated by the enormous room with its heavy, masculine furniture and wealth of priceless-looking artwork. A large marble fireplace anchored the west wall below a mantle that held a collage of photos and abstract sculptures. He wondered if they all would eventually fall victim to Silas's rage.

A familiar picture caught his eye. A teenage Harper sat atop a chestnut-colored horse with a long blond mane. She wore a cowboy hat, a fringed leather vest, and the same light in her eyes that Silas had referred to. Harper kept a copy of the same picture at her apartment. His vision blurred, and he wiped his eyes.

He picked up the Christmas photo of Silas and Harper. This one he hadn't seen before, and it caused a tsunami of emotion. Unprepared for such an assault, he sat on the edge of a leather chair in the middle of the room. Zac shook his head as he stared at her face in the photo.

Suddenly and unexpectedly, a sharp pain snaked its way between his eyes. He flinched and dropped the picture. The pain increased and he grabbed the arm of the chair for support. Harper stared up at him from the floor. As he reached for her, his world turned black.

The first thing he saw when his sight returned was the inside of his office, but from a strange vantage point. Instead of the leather chair beneath him, he found himself sitting on Rachel's desk. His hands were empty. Silas's picture was nowhere in sight. He squeezed his eyes shut to chase away the lingering pain and try to make sense of what just happened.

The sound of someone unlocking the door interrupted his thoughts. Before he could react, Myles stuck his head in the room and looked around. He stopped when he saw Zac. His brow furrowed as he stared.

Zac waited until the silence became uncomfortable.

"Uh... I was just..." he gave a dismissing wave of his hand. "Long story. What do you need?"

Myles stepped inside. "I heard noise in here as I walked by the door, and I wanted to make sure everything was all right."

Zac glanced around the room, still shaken by the TRD's malfunction. "Everything is... peachy." He forced a smile.

"Peachy?" Myles raised an eyebrow. "What are you doing up there?"

Zac didn't have time to chat, he needed to figure out what went wrong and fix it in a hurry. "Just working through a problem. Sometimes, I need a different perspective." He patted the desktop next to where he sat.

"Anything I can help with?"

"Thanks, but I've got it covered."

Myles shrugged. "OK. You do you. I'm just glad you're working again."

Zac's feet hit the floor as soon as Myles left. He paced around the room, baffled by the TRD's errant behavior. Not only had this been the worst malfunction yet, he failed to get the proof that Silas needed to fund his project. He would have to convince Myles that it was too dangerous to jump again without making some expensive program modifications.

Zac climbed into the backseat of the limo for a second time. The Plexiglass screen rose as they left the curb.

Silas raised an eyebrow. "Well?"

"I don't have it."

"Then why are we here?"

"Look, I told you that it wasn't safe. I tried. It didn't work."

"Try harder."

"I need money to do that."

"You said you tried. Tell me exactly what happened."

Zac paused, deciding how much to tell him. He needed to make it clear that traveling without further programming was reckless. "Nothing worked right. I landed in a pantry, nowhere near my intended destination."

"Let me get this straight. You were in my house on the agreed upon date?"

"Yes, but—"

"Were you ever in my office?"

"Yes, I—"

"Did you see the picture?"

"I did. I had it in my hand when the machine malfunctioned and sent me to the top of my assistant's desk on campus. I don't know where it got those coordinates." As soon as he said it, he remembered the early experiments with the rat. "I'm lucky it didn't send me to the middle of the Charles River. It needs more work."

"The picture." Silas moved closer to the edge of his seat. "What happened to the picture?"

"I dropped it just before I was sent back to the present."

"Near the leather chair in my office?"

Zac saw where this was going. "Yes. I was sitting in the chair when my head exploded." He raised his brow over a triumphant smile. "There's your proof. You found that picture on the floor halfway across the room, unsure of how it got there."

He nodded. "Until now."

"It's not safe to travel without further modifications."

Silas sat back and stared out the window for a moment. "I want you to come work for me."

Zac didn't see that one coming. "What?"

"You'll have your own state-of-the-art lab and a six-figure salary." He turned to Zac and waited for an answer.

As exciting as that sounded, he wasn't ready to work for anyone, especially Silas Gray. He didn't trust the man. It appeared he might be after more than the return of his daughter.

"I appreciate the offer, but I'm going to have to decline."

"I don't understand. You'll have access to whatever resources you need. I thought that's what you wanted."

"We both want Harper back. Sixty thousand dollars will make that happen. Let's just stick to the plan."

Silas frowned, then produced a checkbook and silver pen from the inside pocket of his suit jacket. He scribbled in the book for a moment, tore off a check, and handed it to Zac. The whirring sound returned as the Plexiglass screen retracted.

"Take us back to the auditorium."

Zac stared at the eighty-thousand-dollar check in his hand. "I only asked for sixty."

"Consider it an advance on your future employment."

Sneaky bastard! Zac couldn't cash the check for only sixty thousand. He'd have to accept it all.

"I haven't agreed to anything beyond bringing Harper back."

"Do you want the money, or don't you?"

The limo slipped back into a parking spot near the auditorium. Zac stepped out and watched it glide away as smoothly as if the tires never touched the pavement. The money had strings attached. He didn't like strings. He'd been looking for an angel. What he found was something entirely different.

Zac shoved the check into his shirt pocket. He would deposit it on Monday. In the meantime, he would make a few calls and green light the project.

CHAPTER 22

Rachel crashed on her sofa, the television on low so she didn't feel alone in her apartment. She poured herself another glass of wine. Since her surgery, she'd been reluctant to imbibe more than a small glass of champagne at New Year's Eve. Her doctor had warned that too much alcohol would be dangerous when mixed with her medication. Tonight, she didn't care. What was the point? Her number had come up a year ago, and she'd fought it kicking and screaming. Why? So she could live to betray a man who'd done nothing wrong? A man who struggled with his own demons? A man for whom she had feelings?

Myles had called her into his office again to squeeze her for more information. Hadn't she done enough? She loathed herself for her betrayal. Myles demanded that she *do whatever it takes* to get close enough to Zac that he might reveal the intimate details of his project. That's not how she understood their agreement. She didn't know how far she could go or how long she could keep up her reluctant charade.

She really screwed up today. The look of confusion and betrayal in Zac's eyes broke her heart. He may never trust her again. Why did she even care? This was a temporary assignment. Move to Boston for a few months to learn everything she can about the woman who saved her life. Zachary Taylor wasn't even on her radar. If it hadn't been for Harper's father, she wouldn't know that Zac existed. She wondered if they might both be better off.

Rachel poured another glass and turned up the volume on the television. A couple searched for a house in Costa Rica on one of those Home & Garden channels. She'd give anything to be in Costa Rica, no longer under the thumb of Myles Gordon. A picture of Zac and her on a white sand beach floated through her mind. Embarrassed, she shook it away.

She picked up her journal and wrote about her feelings, careful not to mention the beach. She'd been writing since she was a little girl and had a stack of journals to prove it. Being a private person didn't mean her head wasn't full of thoughts and opinions. It just meant she wasn't comfortable sharing them with others. She had been through hell, in and out of hospitals, and lived to tell about it. Maybe someday she would write her memoir.

After a couple more glasses of wine and several infomercials, Charlie scratched at the door. Rachel stood, her head light and her limbs heavy. Was she tired or drunk? She'd forgotten what the latter felt like. Unable to take her dog for a walk, she let him out and returned to the sofa. The dead weight of her body compressed the soft centers of the cushions. The edges reached up around her like a warm hug. Sleep came swiftly.

Dreams, as vivid as they were bizarre, played out in her restless mind. At one point, she became Dorothy in the Wizard of Oz, following the yellow-brick road with Charlie in her basket and Zac, a.k.a. the scarecrow, at her side. They searched for something. No, someone. They had set off to find the great and powerful wizard, whom they'd been told could help them.

She lost Zac along the way. Frightened and alone, she eventually fought her way into the palace of the wizard, where she fell to her knees before a twenty-foot, fire-breathing apparition of Myles Gordon. But instead of helping her, he scolded and threatened her. Turning to flee, she spied a man's feet barely visible behind a large velvet curtain. She pulled back the curtain to find a wild-eyed Silas Gray pushing levers and pulling ropes.

Rachel awoke to her own muffled screams, her clothes soaked with sweat. Light from the television flickered around the room. A mild pain radiated from her chest while another throbbed in her head. She shuffled into the kitchen and swallowed a couple of pain pills before returning to the comfort of the sofa cushions.

Sleep was light and dreaming spotty. In the most vivid scene, she found herself in an operating room. A bright overhead light bathed the operating table until a surgeon leaned over her body. He held out his hand and called for a scalpel. Rachel panicked. I'm still awake, she thought. Where's the anesthesia? She called out for the doctor to stop, but she had no voice.

The surgeon's face hid behind a mask, but the eyes gave him away. Myles Gordon plunged the knife into her chest. She tried to scream in pain, but a low, muffled sound was all she managed. A fire burned in her chest, and she thought it might melt the rest of her internal organs. She rocked her body back and forth so violently that she rolled off the sofa onto the floor.

Rachel opened her eyes. TV lights flickered and strange voices filled the room. The burning persisted and kept her from sitting. She reached up and ran her hand across the top of the coffee table until she found her phone. It fell to the floor in front of her. She stabbed at three numbers, hoping her voice had returned.

"9-1-1, what's your emergency?"

"I'm having a heart attack!"

Chapter 23

Zac stopped at the bank on the way to work Monday morning and left with renewed enthusiasm. A major roadblock had been removed. He couldn't wait to talk to Harper again in the flesh. He had spoken to her many times over the past year, but it had been more of a monologue than an actual conversation.

The coffee shop had been busier than usual, and the morning passed quickly. Myles stopped by shortly after Zac arrived on campus, asking too many questions about what he was working on. He never mentioned Rachel, unaware that she'd been unilaterally suspended for her attempted espionage.

Zac had a difficult time maintaining a sufficient level of concentration as the afternoon wore on. Thoughts of Rachel slipped in and out uncontrollably. He wondered where she was and what she might be doing with her free time. He missed the secret glances he threw her way when she wasn't looking and the light in her smile when she was.

He cursed Myles for putting her in such an impossible position. She didn't deserve any of it. Zac may have overreacted when he caught her at his desk. Now, he wanted things to go back to the way they were a week ago. He hoped she felt the same way.

He picked up the phone and dialed her number but hung up after the first ring. What kind of message would that send? She committed a crime; she had to do the time. He pushed the phone away and returned to work. Fifteen minutes later, he had the phone in his hand again. After four rings, it went to voicemail. A flicker of a smile flashed on his lips when he heard her voice.

"Uh… Hi… I could use some help around here. So… I guess it would be okay if you come back to work tomorrow." He waited for a few seconds before setting the phone down, but before it reached the cradle, he pulled it back to his ear. "It's Zac." An awkward pause followed. "Bye."

Zac hated voice mail, or answering machines as he still called it. He tried to put her out of his mind and get back to work. Before he left for the night, he called her again, and again she didn't answer. This time, he hung up without leaving a message.

Tuesday was Zac's day off at the coffee shop, so he would put in a full day on campus. On the way to school, he stopped for coffee and bagels to go. Hopefully, Rachel would be back to work today. He wanted to be angry at her, but those feelings had been short-lived. She still needed to regain his trust, but he was willing to give her the opportunity.

A sudden wave of guilt swept over him. He needed to stay focused on his goal. Rachel had become a distraction, a pleasant one perhaps, but he couldn't let anyone or anything impede his progress. The light at the end of this tunnel was Harper Gray. Period. End of story.

Rachel sat up in bed for the first time in two days. She'd been heavily sedated, and her memory of the events leading up to her current predicament was unreliable. She spent most of the first day weaving her way in and out of consciousness while the hospital staff pumped her full of steroids and antibiotics. Her head cleared a bit the second day, but her memories consisted mostly of being fed by a nurse and a couple of trips to the bathroom.

A nurse propped her head with a pillow and filled her water glass after moving her from the CCU into a private room.

"If you need anything else, just push the call button."

"Where's Charlie?"

"Charlie?"

"My dog. Charlie."

"I don't know, dear. I'll see if they have any information at the desk."

Not what she wanted to hear, but it would have to do for now.

The nurse turned to leave.

"Where are my things?"

She turned. "Everything you came in with is in the closet. Would you like me to get them for you?"

Rachel nodded.

The nurse retrieved a large plastic bag with Rachel's name written on one side in black marker. She deposited it on the bed.

Rachel opened the bag and pawed through the contents. "Where's my phone?"

The nurse shrugged. "That's everything."

"When can I see the doctor?" she asked.

"He'll be here shortly to check on you."

"I need to find my phone."

"I'll see what I can do." The nurse turned and left.

Rachel looked around the room, feeling the weight of her poor choices. She knew better than to drink an entire bottle of wine. She needed two things right now—her phone so she could let someone know where she was, and she needed to know what happened to Charlie. Actually, there were three things. She needed Myles Gordon to go to hell.

Doctor Sommer entered the room and picked up her chart. Rachel expected to see one of the hospital staff doctors, which would give her time to prepare her defense before the inevitable follow-up appointment with her cardiologist. Usually friendly and talkative, Doctor Sommer said nothing while he studied the results of her lab work.

"Did I have a heart attack?"

"Not exactly, though it may have felt like one."

"What happened?"

He looked up from the chart. "I think you know what happened."

Rachel avoided his eyes.

"This is serious, Rachel. You know the rules."

"Yes, but—"

"No buts. It's only been a year since your transplant. You're not out of the woods yet. You're on some powerful medications that don't play well with alcohol and caffeine. The results, as you can see, can be disastrous."

If Rachel told him she didn't care anymore, he might order a psych evaluation. She said nothing.

Doctor Sommer finished his lecture, then informed Rachel that she needed to stay in the hospital for a couple of days for observation.

When he left, Rachel buried her head in the pillow.

The nurse returned a few minutes later. "I'm sorry, but no one has seen your phone. And I checked with the EMTs who brought you in. You were alone in the house when they arrived."

Rachel drilled down a little deeper into the pillow. *And the hits just keep on coming!*

CHAPTER 24

Zac unlocked the door and set a bag on Rachel's desk and another on his. He tinkered with a few things, but his mind was somewhere else. He finished his coffee and dropped half a bagel back in the bag. The clock on the wall showed 9:00 the first time he looked, then 9:15, then 9:30. Rachel's coffee would be cold by now.

At 9:40, he dialed Rachel's number and left a brief message reminding her she could return to work. Was she turning the tables, punishing him for the way he treated her? He hadn't given her a chance to explain herself. She'd been tried and convicted with no opportunity for a proper defense. He berated himself for not handling the situation differently.

By eleven o'clock, he'd had enough. Zac wasted the entire morning worrying about a woman he had no business worrying about. He should have spent his time thinking about how to transport his sorry ass back in time to save Harper. Harper Gray? Remember her?

Zac locked up his office and set off to get some fresh air. He walked down to the Student Center, where he'd eaten lunch on occasion. Sometimes, he'd go down there to clear his head. Rachel had suggested it once when he'd hit a wall after hours of intense concentration in the physics lab. Of course, he'd resisted at first, that is until he tried it. It seemed she'd known him better than he thought.

The distraction helped, but not enough. He tried sitting in one of the open areas to watch people come and go. Twice, he thought he saw Rachel. The first time, he stood to get a better look. The second time, he chased after her, only to embarrass himself in front of a perfect stranger.

The lunch crowd rolled in, and the smell of food that drifted out into the open spaces drew Zac into the food court. He bought a sandwich and headed back to the office. The warm air made a case for eating his lunch outside, but he'd wasted enough of the day. He would eat while he worked.

A small dog that resembled Charlie sat by the door to his building. He appeared to be waiting for someone. Zac stopped and called out, "Charlie."

The dog's head snapped in his direction before he broke into a run. Zac bent down to meet Charlie at his level. He wasn't sure what to do, and he wasn't about to pick the thing up. He'd seen Rachel scratch behind Charlie's ears, so he tried it. Charlie's tail moved back and forth like a metronome on steroids. Even he knew it was a good sign. Okay, that was easy enough.

The dog sniffed around his sandwich bag. Zac moved it to his other hand. The dog followed. Zac held his arm out a few feet off the ground, and Charlie jumped for it twice before he barked.

"Shhh!" Zac looked around for Rachel but came up empty. "Fine! We can share. Inside."

Zac scooped him up awkwardly with his free hand and went inside. He Googled, '*What do dogs eat?*', a little embarrassed that he didn't know the answer to such a fundamentally simple question. Satisfied that a little roast beef and bread wouldn't hurt him, he unwrapped his sandwich, and the two ate lunch together. Charlie acted like he hadn't eaten in a while.

Charlie drank water from a paper plate almost as fast as Zac could pour it. Zac opened Rachel's bottom desk drawer and deposited his dinner guest inside after he'd had his fill. He sat down in Rachel's chair and watched Charlie for a moment, confused about how and why he was here when there was no sign of Rachel anywhere. It made no sense. The two had been inseparable since the first day she brought him in. He thought about bursting into Myles's office and demanding to know what he'd done with her. He eventually thought better of it, at least until he had a little more information.

As the day wore on with no sign of Rachel, and Zac's repeated calls went unanswered, his worry meter entered the red zone. He barely made it to three o'clock before he packed up his things, scooped Charlie up from his drawer, and set off to find her.

That's what any good boss would do, isn't it? A good boss knew some basic information about his employees, but Zac knew virtually nothing about Rachel, including where she lived. He made a mental note to fix that when he found her.

Zac called Myles's secretary for Rachel's address. He donned an oversized lab coat, tucked Charlie inside, and boarded a bus for Strawberry Hill. Rachel lived in a duplex in a nice, middle-class neighborhood. Two young children played in the yard next door. He wondered how long she'd lived there, and where she'd grown up.

Charlie barked as soon as they reached the front porch. Zac found Rachel's name under one of the doorbells and stabbed the button. He set Charlie down. The dog's back stiffened, and he forced a long, low growl through clenched teeth. Zac had never seen him so agitated. He opened the screen door and pounded on the inner door. Charlie barked again.

Zac peeked inside between the curtains. What he saw made him uneasy. The coffee table in her living room sat at an awkward angle, like it had been pushed or kicked away from the sofa. Several items were strewn around it on the floor. He pulled his phone from his pocket and dialed Rachel's number. A phone rang inside the apartment. Charlie barked.

The door to the other apartment opened a few inches. "She's not home," a fifty-something woman said in a tentative voice.

"Do you know where she is?"

The door closed a little as Zac approached. "Who wants to know?"

"I'm her boss. She hasn't been to work for a couple of days."

She swung the door wide. "Thank goodness. I didn't know who to contact. She's a nice enough girl, but she doesn't talk much about herself, so I didn't know—"

"Did something happen? Is she alright?"

Charlie's ears stood up like he understood our conversation, but he remained silent for the moment.

"Yes..." she said, then shook her head, "and I don't know."

Zac ran his fingers back through his hair. "Just tell me what you know."

"An ambulance came a few nights ago. They made such a racket."

"Do you know where they took her?"

She shook her head. "They weren't here long, and they left in a hurry."

Zac scratched the space above his lip, fearing the worst.

"Is that her little dog?"

He glanced at Charlie. "Yes, it is. Why?"

"Didn't know if they left him inside. I didn't hear anything, but he's pretty quiet most of the time."

Zac shifted his weight from one foot to the other like the porch was on fire. "Did you notice anything about the ambulance? Was there a name on the side?"

"It was dark. I didn't see a name, but I think it was red and white."

Pretty much every ambulance in the country is red and white. "Where's the nearest emergency room?"

"That's easy. Mount Auburn is about five minutes away."

Zac thanked her for her help, then set off on foot with Charlie close behind.

CHAPTER 25

Zac walked up to the Information Desk at Mount Auburn Hospital with Charlie tucked inside his coat.

"Can you tell me what room Rachel Lockhart is in?"

"Let me see..." A receptionist with tired eyes stared at the computer screen in front of her. "She's in our Coronary Unit. Third floor. Room 311."

Charlie squirmed, and Zac made an awkward adjustment.

The nurse studied him for a moment. "Elevator is down the hall on the right."

Zac found Room 311 and took a deep breath before he stepped inside. Rachel sat in her bed, watching Doctor Phil on the wall-mounted television. Her face lit up when Zac walked in.

"Oh my God, Zac. I'm so glad to see you. How did you find me?"

Zac sat on the end of the bed and unbuttoned the top button of his lab coat. Charlie's head poked out. "You mean how did *we* find you."

Rachel's eyes widened and her mouth opened. Zac unbuttoned another button, and Charlie jumped out and into Rachel's waiting arms. She squeezed him like a little girl squeezes her favorite doll. Before she let go, she looked up at Zac with tearful eyes and mouthed, *thank you*.

Eventually, she loosened her grip, and Charlie curled up in her lap.

"Where did you... how..." She paused to collect herself. "How did you find him?"

"He found me." Zac shrugged. "He was sitting in front of the building when I got back from lunch."

"On campus?" She covered her mouth with her hand. "I let him out Saturday night before any of this happened." She paused. "Zac, I live four miles from campus."

"If you'd answer your phone once in a while, I might have saved him the trip."

Rachel glanced at Charlie with sad eyes, then back to Zac, ignoring his attempt at sarcasm. "Was he okay when you found him?"

"He was pretty hungry. We had lunch." Zac smiled. "By the way, he's quite fond of roast beef sandwiches."

A smile flickered across her lips before her expression fell. "I lost my phone when they brought me here. I would have called to let you know I couldn't come to work."

"Relax. It's still at your apartment."

She frowned. "How do you know that?"

"I called you from your front porch. I heard it ring inside."

"Thank God." She exhaled then raised an eyebrow. "You were at my apartment?"

His cheeks flushed. "Uh... you were A.W.O.L." His eyes drifted for a moment. "Think of it as a boss checking up on his favorite employee." Truth is, he cared about her more than he liked to admit.

They lingered there for a moment in silence.

Rachel looked at Charlie. "I'm his only employee."

Zac smiled, shifting his weight on the bed. "So, what happened?"

Rachel avoided his gaze, scratching behind Charlie's ears. "It was nothing."

"Nothing? This isn't a hotel. You lost your phone and your dog."

"Oh, that." She continued grooming Charlie. "They thought I had a heart attack, but I didn't."

"What do *you* think?" He waited for a reply that never came. "Who called the ambulance?"

"Zac, please. I don't want to talk about it."

"Well, I do." Zac rubbed the back of his neck. "Are you sick?"

"No." She paused. "I had heart surgery a year ago. Saturday night, I had chest pains. I didn't want to take any chances, so I called 911. Turns out, it's nothing serious."

"You had heart surgery? Why?"

She avoided his eyes. "It was a genetic defect. I'm better now."

"This is what better looks like?"

"Please, Zac, don't make a big deal out of nothing."

An awkward silence descended upon the room.

"So... how long do you have to stay in here?"

"A couple more days, according to the doctor."

"I guess I could take care of Charlie until you get back on your feet."

"Thank you, Zac."

He shrugged it off like it was no big deal.

"He's a wonderful dog. He won't be any trouble."

"Of course, you'll owe me big time," he said, only half kidding.

Her raised eyebrow came with no comment. "Come here," she said, with open arms.

Zac approached slowly.

"Thank you," she whispered in his ear as they embraced.

Zac closed his eyes, overcome by feelings he hadn't felt in over a year—an energetic connection with the intensity of lovers that he'd thought only possible with Harper. This confused him, and he disengaged.

He scooped up Charlie. "I better be going."

"Wait."

Zac's embarrassment kept him moving toward the door. Had he violated some forbidden level of intimacy with Rachel, or perhaps a betrayal of his beloved Harper? He had no idea how Rachel felt, or what went through her head at the moment. He might be better off not knowing.

Rachel stared at nothing in particular as she rubbed the scar on her chest through the hospital gown. What troubled her wasn't anything a doctor could fix. Zac had become a good friend, yet she continued to deceive him at every turn. He would never know her biggest secret, the reason she sat in a hospital bed.

She'd listened to him talk about his deceased fiancé on more than a few occasions. She never mentioned that one year ago her life had been saved with a heart donated by a woman who died in the same car accident that ruined his life. She felt Harper Gray's heart beat inside her chest. How could she tell him now?

She never intended to get this involved in Zac's life. She didn't know him when she came to Boston to learn more about her heart donor. A few inquiries or a brief encounter under false pretenses could have satisfied someone else's curiosity. But she needed more.

After all, what's in a person's heart made them who they are. Losing hers had left her adrift. Now, she had a new heart donated by a virtual stranger. Rachel no longer knew who she was or what made her tick. Learning everything she could about Harper Gray was not just a curiosity, it was a burning desire, a priority above all others.

Her condition had kept her from having any serious relationships. She'd felt like damaged goods, unwilling to burden someone else with her affliction. So, she needed to learn more about the man that had captured Harper's heart.

She didn't like Zac all that much when they first met, and it appeared the feeling was mutual. He treated her like a second-class citizen. Why? Because she had an I.Q. below 150? But working with him appeared to have changed him as much as it changed her. She'd seen glimpses of vulnerability and even compassion. When he walked into her room with Charlie, she'd wanted to kiss him, but that would be crossing a line she was unprepared to cross.

Chapter 26

Zac needed to focus. Every hour away from his project represented an hour lost with Harper. With Charlie tucked away in his drawer, he checked on the progress of the programming he'd farmed out to three local firms. The coding requirements had been divided and distributed so no single person or firm had enough of the work to determine the functionality of the final product. Zac's excitement grew with each project status report he reviewed. All three modules were complete and ready to download from a secure site.

Unable to offer his staff's services, Zac's friend in the IT Department hand-picked two of the best and brightest from a group of interns to work on the last piece, which would be completed by the end of the day.

Something rubbed against Zac's leg. Startled, he kicked at it. Charlie yipped and scampered out from under the desk. He stared at Zac with such big, sad eyes that Zac picked him up and set him on his lap. Why did he offer to take care of the dog in the first place? He rolled his eyes, knowing the answer to his question.

Zac set Charlie back in his drawer and returned to work. He updated the firmware with the three completed modules and made plans for his trip. Unfortunately, he didn't have all the necessary information. What he had, came from memory. The events of that night were blurry, his memories unreliable. He'd tried meditation and self-hypnosis with limited success.

He knew the date and location of the accident, but the exact time eluded him. It had been a meaningless detail. His research turned up two newspaper articles. Neither listed the time of the accident. He filed a Freedom of Information request and received a barely legible copy of the police report. Not much help there.

The trip would have to wait until after the final program update. Rachel had been on Zac's mind most of the morning. A visit to the hospital to pass the time sounded like a good way to keep his mind off the insufferable waiting.

Myles poked his head in the door as Zac bent down to pick up Charlie.

"Sorry, Charlie," Zac whispered and quickly closed the drawer.

"We were supposed to meet yesterday."

Zac had been avoiding Myles. "Sorry about that. Rachel's in the hospital, and I went to visit her."

"The hospital?" He blinked back his surprise. "What happened?"

"Nobody's sure. Something with her heart."

"Is she okay?"

"I think so." Zac hoped his excuse would be enough to send him on his way. It wasn't.

Myles pulled a paper from the folder under his arm and handed it to Zac. "What's this?"

Zac studied the invoice from one of the programming firms he'd hired. They sent the bill to the school by mistake. Unable to tell Myles the truth, he had no other plausible explanation. "It's nothing you need to worry about. I'll take care of it."

For a moment, neither of them said anything.

Zac folded the paper and shoved it into his back pocket. He needed to change the subject. "I was on my way out to visit Rachel. I'll tell her you said hello."

"Not so fast." Myles folded his arms across his chest. "I have a couple of questions."

Zac didn't have any answers, at least not any he'd be willing to share with Myles. He needed time to think. "Can we do this some other time?"

"I'm afraid not."

"I said, I'll take care of it."

"What's it for?"

"Some high-end programming that I didn't think I could do myself."

"It says you paid a five-thousand-dollar down payment, and they're looking for five more." He frowned. "You don't have that kind of money."

"It's not your problem."

"Everything you do is my problem now."

Zac bristled. Fine. I'll pack up my shit and get the hell out of here. Problem solved." He didn't need Myles's charity anymore. Tomorrow, he would travel back and prevent the accident. He might even roll the dice and stay there, reliving the past year with Harper. There's a good chance he might never see Myles Gordon again.

Zac watched fear and confusion cloud Myles's arrogant eyes. Myles needed him to stay. What Zac didn't know was why.

Myles held up his hands. "Let's just take a breath. I never said anything about leaving."

They stood in silence, letting the intensity of their conversation settle.

"I came down here to check on your progress," Myles said, "and to see if there was anything else you needed from me."

An obvious lie. Fortunately, Zac hadn't mentioned anything to anyone about the TRD. As far as Myles knew, Zac had been working on his theory for teleportation. Had Myles seen through Zac's duplicity? Is that why he hired Rachel? What had she told him?

If Zac went public with either of his inventions, the potential economic implications would be staggering. Perhaps Myles's gambling problem had landed him in trouble again, and he looked at Zac as his ticket out.

Zac's threat had shut Myles down for the time being. He would give him a little morsel of information and send him on his way. "I'm still shaking a few bugs out of my theory, particularly in the location language, but it looks promising." He paused. "I couldn't have gotten this far without your support, Myles."

"My pleasure." He smiled an uncertain smile. "We make a good team, don't we?"

Zac nodded. "Indeed, we do."

Myles patted him on the back and left the room fat, dumb, and happy. Zac congratulated himself for how he handled the situation. He opened Rachel's desk drawer to give Charlie some air.

"Sorry about that, boy, but we can't let mean old Uncle Myles find you in the office." Zac sat in Rachel's chair with Charlie on his lap. Charlie's tail tapped against his leg as the dog watched him intently. Zac met his gaze. "We're going to have to watch our backs from now on, aren't we?"

Zac shook his head. Look at yourself, he thought. You're having a conversation with a dog. He had to admit, Charlie was a good listener.

Zac scooped the dog up into his arms and stood. "Come on, Charlie. Time to find out exactly what Rachel told mean old Uncle Myles."

Chapter 27

Zac dropped Charlie off at his apartment. He set out two bowls. One he filled with water and the other with dog food he'd bought on the way home the day before. He warned Charlie to behave before heading for the hospital.

Rachel greeted him with a smile, and he sat on the end of the bed as he had done on his previous visit.

"Where's Charlie?" she asked.

Zac smiled and held his arms out at his sides. "What about... *Hi Zac, nice to see you again?*"

"I'm sorry. Hi Zac, nice to see you again." She snickered. "Where's Charlie?"

"I didn't want to risk getting both of us thrown out, so I left him home."

Rachel's eyes widened. "Alone?"

"No. Your friend Amy is watching him."

"Amy?"

"Your friend. Amy. The one who lives in my building. You must remember her. You came to my building looking for her."

"Oh... that Amy."

He sensed a note of distress in her voice, and a sinister smile crossed his lips. "I asked her about you when I dropped Charlie off."

Rachel let out a nervous laugh. "Uh... we weren't that close. She probably wouldn't remember me."

Zac watched her squirm. "We both know you weren't there to see your imaginary friend, Amy." He folded his arms across his chest. "What were you doing on my porch?"

The words hung in the air between them, and she bit her lower lip.

"Did Myles send you?"

"Myles?" She frowned. "I didn't even know who Myles Gordon was back then."

"You know him now, and I'm pretty sure he told you to spy on me."

"I don't know what you're talking about." She pulled her sheet up and busied herself tucking it here and there.

"Give it up, Rachel. I overheard the two of you in Myles's office the other day. Myles wasn't happy. Your spying skills need some work."

Rachel hung her head. "I'm sorry, Zac. I didn't have a choice."

"Everyone has a choice."

"That's easy for you to say. I needed a job. I figured Myles needed a babysitter for one of his eggheads. No offense. Whatever information I might give him was just some benign academic mumbo jumbo that I couldn't even begin to understand."

"I trusted you. I just don't know how you could have done something like that."

"It was easy at first. You were a real tool."

"Is it easy now?"

"No." She wiped a tear that clung to her chin. "It's very difficult."

Zac second-guessed getting into all this in the hospital, but patience wasn't his strong suit. He felt betrayed. It's possible he was more upset with himself for getting too close to someone again.

Her tears had an unexpected effect. But not as unexpected as what happened next. Zac leaned a little closer and wiped the tears from her eyes. Rachel put her head on his shoulder, and Zac couldn't fight the urge to hold her and comfort her.

"I'm sorry, Zac," she whispered.

He didn't know how to respond. Not only was he out of his element, the feeling he'd had the last time they were this close returned. This time, he didn't turn and run.

Rachel raised her head and wiped a tear. "I never intended to hurt you." She reeked of sincerity.

A novice like Zac didn't stand a chance against those eyes. His formidable brain turned to mush. "Good, because I really want to kiss you."

She hesitated.

The silence sobered him, and he wished he could take his words back. "Say something."

"If you did... I wouldn't turn away," she said in a voice as soft as an angel.

He leaned in. Her warm, soft lips tasted of tears. Feelings that had remained dormant for over a year awoke inside him. They confused him and made it difficult to think clearly. He came here for information, not for whatever this was.

The moment came and went, and they both looked away, embarrassed. Their eyes met again. These were not the eyes of a spy. Nevertheless, he'd come here on a mission. He could work on damage control once she came clean, so they could put this unfortunate incident behind them.

Zac stood. He paced in front of the bed.

"What?"

"I need to know what you told Myles."

"Please, Zac. Not now." She closed her eyes and shook her head. "I'll tell you everything when I get out of here."

He wouldn't hold a gun to her head. Not now. "Fine. When are they letting you out?"

"I'll be home tomorrow afternoon."

He nearly bent to kiss her goodbye on his way out. *Get a grip, Zac.*

Zac spent the first part of the afternoon installing a webcam in his office. He didn't know who to trust anymore. Given the sensitive nature of his work, he couldn't take any unnecessary chances. He spent the rest of the afternoon preparing for the next day's jump into the past. The final module had been completed as promised, and he updated the TRD's firmware. The trip will be a test of the modified operating system. Confident that the device will work properly, Operation Save Harper would proceed according to plan.

There was just one problem. He hadn't been able to stop thinking about that moment he and Rachel shared in the hospital. He'd let his feelings get in the way of his work, not something he was accustomed to doing. The work that should have taken two hours had taken four. His lack of concentration eroded his confidence, and he had to recheck everything. *There could be no mistakes this time.*

Tomorrow morning, he will leave his apartment right after breakfast and arrive outside Harper's building at precisely 9 pm. She needed to be stopped before getting into her car and driving off to a fiery crash. Everything was ready. His heart skipped a beat thinking about seeing her again. After he took Charlie for a walk to take care of business, he retired for the night.

Zac slept in fits and starts. He'd had the dream again. The one where he's driving a car backwards and the brakes don't work no matter how hard he pressed the pedal. He figured it had something to do with losing control of his life. That wasn't far from the truth for most of the past year, but he was doing something about it now. He'd regained control, hadn't he? No more feeling sorry for himself. He had a plan.

He rose before his seven o'clock alarm and stood in the shower for a full ten minutes. After a quick breakfast of cold cereal and a morning walk with Charlie, he loaded the new and improved TRD into his backpack and slipped it on. Charlie growled at something outside while Zac went through his preflight checklist.

Zac pushed back the curtain an inch and checked the front of the building. Nothing.

He turned to Charlie. "Stop it."

Charlie continued to growl, throwing in a couple of barks now and then for good measure.

"That's it." He scooped Charlie up. "You're getting locked in the bathroom. I've got important business to attend to, and I don't have time for games."

As Zac took a step toward the bathroom, Charlie struggled. Zac over-compensated, and Charlie's front leg landed hard on the launch button on Zac's wrist.

Man and dog disappeared into the past.

CHAPTER 28

Streetlights burned against a black sky. Zac recognized his surroundings. He'd landed a block away from his intended target. His head throbbed, and he had to close his eyes. Charlie continued to struggle in his arms. Zac loosened his grip, and the dog jumped to the ground.

"Not cool," Zac said to Charlie.

The dog paid no attention, sniffing around at something he'd found near the curb.

"You'd better be on your best behavior. I don't need you screwing up this trip any more than you already have." He shook his head. "Dumb dog."

Charlie looked up at him with a *who-you-calling-dumb* look.

Zac sighed. Disappointed that the location was still off after the programming modifications, he checked the time on his phone. 9:27. His best guess put the accident, which happened three blocks away, at approximately 9:40. He must hurry.

"C'mon, dummy," he called as he walked toward Harper's apartment.

He hadn't gotten ten feet when the sickening sound of metal scraping metal stopped him in his tracks. Zac cringed as if a thousand fingernails dragged across a chalkboard. His head snapped in the direction of the sound.

"Nooo," he screamed.

He looked at the apartment building, then back toward the sound. He'd guessed wrong. Zac broke into a dead run.

"Charlie," he shouted, without breaking stride.

The first time this had happened, he'd been in the apartment, unaware. Eventually, the sirens coaxed him out, but it had been too late. Harper's car had burst into flames. Did she die on impact? Was she trapped inside before the explosion? For how long? Many questions were left unanswered. He'd always held on to the hope that she hadn't suffered. He pushed harder, but he'd reached his top speed.

A sea of brake lights spilled from the next intersection. An imaginary fist punched his side, and he had to stop. He leaned over, hands on his knees, fighting for each breath. Harper's time had nearly run out. He had to push on. Adrenaline coursed through his veins, moving him forward once again.

A crowd had formed a circle around the scene. Zac sliced his way through. He stopped when he reached a clearing. The horrible scene playing out in front of him sucked the little air he had left from his lungs. He saw the top of Harper's head slumped over the steering wheel as firemen hurried to extract her from the crumpled vehicle. Gasoline fumes filled the air, and he pulled his collar up over his nose. A river of liquid fire flowed from the heap of twisted metal.

Pain split his side as he ran toward his worst nightmare. He made it to within twenty feet of her car before a solid wall of hot air, blowing like a tempest from the center of hell, pushed him back and threw him to the ground. He watched the swirling fireball rise into the night air.

Zac lay on the ground, sounds muffled by the tears spilling down the sides of his head and gathering in his ears. A man dropped to one knee beside him and asked if he was alright. He was not alright. He lied, and the good Samaritan pulled him to his feet. Police set up a perimeter, pushing everyone back from the scene. Zac hung his head, unable to watch the fireman tend to the lifeless body they'd pulled from the wreck just before it exploded.

Tears flowed, and Zac wiped them away with the back of his hand. He'd failed miserably. Reliving this tragedy only added insult to injury. What was he doing here? Maybe events of the past are cast in stone and shouldn't be messed with by anyone. Who did he think he was, anyway? He stood there in a sea of humanity, feeling completely and utterly alone.

A blood-curdling scream split the acrid air that shrouded the intersection. People sometimes don't recognize their own voice when they hear it played back for them. There was no mistaking this one. He watched himself, mouth open and eyes wild, push his way through the crowd three feet from where he stood. What if he'd been spotted? What if they'd touched? As curious as his scientific mind was, he didn't care to find out right now.

Zac had seen enough. He pressed the button on his wrist that sent him home.

Rachel watched her landlady unlock her apartment door. She thanked her and assured her she felt much better. The EMTs had wheeled her out of her apartment in a semi-conscious state with nothing but the clothes on her back. Her landlady next door had witnessed everything and locked the door.

Everything looked out of place. She picked up her phone from the floor and plugged it into the charger. Charlie's bowls sat empty on the floor in the kitchen, and she wondered how he'd fared without her. She opened the fridge and threw out the wilted lettuce and a half-gallon of spoiled milk.

After a quick shower to wash the hospital from her body, she checked her phone. Six calls from Zac, three had voicemail messages attached. He didn't like to leave messages, and she giggled after he finished the last one. That enormous brain of his didn't seem so intimidating now. She hated to admit it, but she'd developed a soft spot in her heart for the boy genius.

The smile slid off her face when she remembered that she'd promised to tell Zac about her treasonous activities over the past month. She wished she hadn't admitted anything, but he had her dead to rights. She wasn't very good at this spy game. As much as she dreaded that conversation, she couldn't wait to see her beloved dog again. Zac had been so sweet to smuggle him into the hospital for her.

Rachel picked up the phone and dialed Zac's number. After four rings, it went to voicemail.

"Hi Zac, I'm home now. I can't wait to see my little Charlie again. Call me as soon as you get this."

Chapter 29

Zac barely had the strength to stand when he returned to his apartment. He slipped off his backpack and crashed on the sofa. Tears flowed. He'd unwittingly forced himself to relive the worst day of his life. He wanted to throw the damn TRD off the top of the John Hancock Tower.

His phone rang. Rachel calling. He couldn't talk to her like this. He let it go. Shortly after it stopped ringing, a ping indicated that she'd left a message. Despite his foul mood, Rachel's voice brought a flicker of a smile to his lips. Halfway through the message, his expression fell, and he dropped the phone.

"Charlie!"

This day couldn't get any worse.

He'd failed miserably in his attempt to save Harper. And if that wasn't bad enough, in one day, he'd single-handedly blown up whatever it was he'd had with Rachel. She'd been a nuisance at first, but she possessed some endearing qualities that reminded him of Harper. They'd been through some rough times together and found comfort in each other's company. She'd become a friend, maybe even more than a friend. It didn't matter anymore. He blew it.

Another early morning stroll on the Longfellow Bridge wasn't out of the question. Or maybe he'd pack up what little he owned and hop on the next bus out of town. Uncle Fred had plenty of room. Surely, someone with Zac's superior intelligence could find a job there. He closed his eyes. It had been an exhausting day, and it wasn't even noon.

The phone rang again. Myles asked about Rachel, then suggested Zac take the day off. Zac agreed and asked for the following day, giving him a four-day weekend to recover from his debacle. Myles agreed too easily, causing Zac to question his motives. He ended the call and buried himself deeper into the sofa cushions.

After nearly twenty-four hours, Zac opened his drowsy eyes only to shut them again. This went on for ten minutes. Sunlight streamed through the window, cutting a swath across his upper body. He blinked several times to focus. He sat up and ran his hands back through his hair before he picked up his phone. 10:30. It should be dark, he thought. He sprang from the sofa when he realized it must be Friday morning.

Already late for work at the coffee shop, he called in sick, then fell back into the cushions. The day got off to a dreadful start, so he had to turn it around, hoping it might end better than the day before. He stared at the ceiling, taking stock of his current situation.

The new day brought new challenges, but also new opportunities. He'd never been a quitter, well, almost never, but he wasn't about to give up this mission without a fight. The TRD needed a few more tweaks, and he needed a new game plan. Both doable once he stopped feeling sorry for himself. It's not how many times you get knocked down that count, it's how many times you get back up.

He couldn't fix his next problem as easily. Losing Charlie might be unforgivable. Zac's conflicted heart ached. He'd planned to be there for Rachel and do something nice to help her get back on her feet. Now he wanted to avoid her at all cost.

No! He didn't want to be that guy. He had to face Rachel again and throw himself at her mercy, but he might use her admitted espionage as a bargaining chip.

After a long, hot shower, Zac Googled *chicken soup recipes*, then headed for the market. His culinary skills were nothing to write home about, but how hard could it be to make a pot of soup? They say chicken soup cures anything that ails you. He wasn't sure if his motivation for such a grand gesture had more to do with genuine feelings for her or a peace offering after losing her dog. In either case, he hoped to soften the blow.

Zac spent the next four hours picking up supplies, mixing up his first pot of soup from scratch, and patting himself on the back for his achievement. He'd found a recipe online and used a simple analogy. The ingredients of the soup were the analogues of particles, and the way you mix them together is like the interaction between the particles. Basic physics, he thought.

Rather than wait for the bus with a pot of soup, he ordered an Uber. On the way, he practiced his *I'm-sorry-I-lost-your-dog* speech, a conversation he'd rather not have to suffer through. For a moment, he considered setting the pot down by her door, ringing the bell, and beating a hasty retreat. He asked the driver to stop at a liquor store where he bought a bottle of wine.

Rachel's eyes grew wide when she greeted him at the door, and Zac noticed a flash of fear mixed with her obvious surprise. She had some explaining to do, herself, and it appeared she had an elephant of her own in the room. She invited Zac in, and the four of them stood in her living room.

"Where's Charlie?"

"Here's the thing." Zac avoided her eyes. "I didn't bring him because I wanted you to have a little time to settle in."

"But I miss him," she said with a pout.

"Take the weekend for yourself. I'll bring him to work on Monday."

One elephant made himself comfortable on the sofa.

Rachel's shoulders fell. "I guess I don't have a choice, do I?"

He handed her the bottle.

Rachel hesitated. "Thank you, but—"

"You're welcome." It wasn't a dog, but it was something.

She set the bottle down and folded her arms across her chest. She raised an eyebrow. "What's in the pot?"

"Dinner."

"You brought me dinner?" The muscles in her neck relaxed and a tentative smile crossed her lips. "What is it?"

Zac removed the lid and held the pot out. "Chicken soup," he said with his chin held high.

"I don't have the flu."

"Yes, but I read somewhere that it cures everything."

"Have you been surfing the Internet again?"

"Chicken soup inhibits the movement of neutrophils."

"That's probably more than I need to know." She took the pot and placed it on the stove.

Zac followed her into a kitchen that didn't appear to get much use, the counters bare except for a small coffee machine. He'd pictured it differently. The whole place seemed temporary. Where did she come from, and how long did she plan to stay? It wouldn't matter after Monday.

She set the pot on the stove and turned to him.

"About the Myles thing…" She stared at the floor. "I'm sorry. I know I shouldn't have agreed to it, but I needed the job."

The other elephant left the room while the first one watched from his seat on the sofa. Sadly, he wasn't going anywhere.

"I've given it some thought lately, and I want you to keep your job."

Her lips twitched in a weak smile beneath a raised eyebrow. "You're not mad at me?"

"I didn't say that." He wouldn't let her off the hook that easily. "First, you're going to tell me everything you told Myles. Then we're going to figure out a way to beat him at his own game."

CHAPTER 30

M yles unlocked the door to Zac's office, stepped inside, and locked the door behind himself. With his spy out of commission, he needed to take matters into his own hands. He'd given Zac a couple of days off to make snooping a little less risky. Zac had been less than forthcoming the last time they met. He was hiding something, and Myles needed to know what it was, sooner rather than later.

Pleasantly surprised to find the desk drawers unlocked, he rifled through the top two with no luck. The device he pulled from the bottom drawer resembled a desktop computer with the cover removed. He set it on the desk and studied it, recalling a time before Zac's meltdown when they discussed potential dissertation topics. Zac always got ahead of himself. Myles explained more than once that he didn't actually have to prove something, as long as he could defend his theory, critically analyzing the reasoning and the merit of his scientific method. To which Zac responded, "What better proof than to see it work."

Did this thing work? Was this a prototype teleportation device? That's what Zac needed the money for. But where did the money come from? Did he already have a backer? Myles had offered him support and a place to work, not solely from the goodness of his heart. He wanted—no, he needed—to share in the spoils when Boy Genius's discoveries were brought to market. That had been the plan all along.

A device such as this held enormous military and commercial potential. Soldiers could be deployed to distant battlefields in the time it takes to snap one's fingers. Likewise, commercial air travel with all its undesirable delays and tedious protocols could become a thing of the past—not to mention the positive effects on climate control. The economic and cultural potential was mind-boggling. He could pay off Silas, then tell him to go to hell.

A patent on such technology could make its owner richer than Bill Gates and Warren Buffett combined virtually overnight. Even as Myles's financial situation neared the critical stage, he wouldn't allow himself to entertain the idea of stealing the technology outright. There would be plenty of money to go around. He simply needed to share in the wealth.

He took pictures of the device from every conceivable angle and wrote down the manufacturer and part number of every component. The notes and calculations that Miss Lockhart provided would help fill in the blanks. She could become a liability if Zac agrees to cut him in. He might be forced to let her go when the time comes.

Rachel set the table for two. She sliced a loaf of French bread and set it on the table. The unopened wine bottle remained in the living room where she'd left it. As promised, she came clean about the things Myles had said when he hired her. Zac unbuttoned the top button of his shirt and rubbed the back of his neck. He paced in the small kitchen when she told him about the photos she'd taken.

"Let me get this straight. You had two copies made? One for me, and one for Myles?"

"I'm sorry, Zac."

He punched his fist into his palm. Rachel jumped. "Is that everything?"

Rachel didn't have the courage to tell him about the box. She nodded, tears rolling off her face onto the kitchen floor.

Zac relaxed a bit. "Good. If that's all he's got, he can't do much with it. Frankly, he's not that smart."

Rachel continued to cry.

Zac surprised her by putting his arm around her shoulder to comfort her. He suggested they table their conversation until after dinner.

Except for some small talk, they ate in silence for the first few minutes.

Zac watched her. "Well?"

"I thought we were going to eat first." She bit her lower lip. Maybe he knew everything she'd done and was testing her.

"How's the soup?"

Rachel paused, surprised at how good the soup tasted. A faint smile played on her lips. "Don't quit your day job."

"Is it that bad?"

"No, it's... it's perfect. Thank you."

Despite the dark cloud that still hung in the air above them, they slipped back into a comfortable groove. After dinner, she washed while he dried. Zac handed her the towel when they finished. Their hands touched, and a slight shiver spread up one arm and down the other. Embarrassed, Rachel slowly let her hand drift away like nothing had happened. His eyes told her otherwise. She took the towel from him and playfully swiped it across his shoulder.

Really, Rachel? That was so middle school.

They still had more to talk through, even though the night seemed headed in an unexpected, but not unwelcome, direction. She needed a drink to take the edge off. Not an entire bottle. That had been a mistake. One small glass couldn't hurt. She poured two glasses, and they moved into the living room.

"What's this?" Zac picked up one of her journals she'd inadvertently left on the sofa.

Rachel panicked. She reached for it. "It's nothing."

He stood and held it up in the air. "Really?"

She jumped up and down, reaching for it.

"It doesn't look like *nothing*."

"Zac, please..." She folded her arms across her chest. "It's personal, so I'd appreciate it if you just stop being such a jackass and give it to me."

"If you tell me what it is, you can have it."

"Fine. It's my journal."

Zac lowered his hand. "You mean like a diary?"

"Something like that." She grabbed the journal and tucked it under her arm.

"Read it to me."

She blushed like a schoolgirl. She'd written Zac's name on more than a few pages. Her expression fell when she realized Harper's was in there as well. "Maybe someday I'll write a book."

Zac raised an eyebrow. "Seriously?"

Rachael placed her hands on her hips. "You don't think I could write a book?"

"About what?"

"I've been writing things down since I was a little girl. I'm sure there's some interesting material. There are a lot of things you don't know about me."

"Tell me one."

She needed to close the door she'd opened with her last remark. "I'm afraid you'll have to wait for the book."

Zac studied her for a moment. He smiled like he'd pushed enough buttons for now. "I'll expect a signed copy."

That was close. She would have to be more careful in the future. Rachel left the room and returned without the journal.

They sipped their drinks in silence. Rachel turned her glass in her hand and watched the wheels of Zac's brain spin. He finished his glass, and she poured him another. She hoped the alcohol would take off more than just the edge. He might go easier on her in a relaxed state.

"Is there anything you need to tell me?" he asked.

Or not. "No." Her voice cracked a little. "I told you everything." More lies. She hated this.

He walked to the table near the front door, pulled his laptop from his backpack, and returned to his seat. "So, you're pretty sure you won't be in the video feed from the office webcam?"

She swallowed hard and did a quick review of her covert activities. Nothing sneaky since she photographed the contents of the box. She prayed that took place before he installed the camera. If it hadn't, she'd have been better off coming clean when he asked about it.

She hesitated. "I'm sure." She loathed herself at the moment.

Zac opened the app and stared at his screen in his lap. His eyes grew wide, and Rachel leaned in to get a better view. They watched in silence as Myles pulled something from Zac's desk drawer.

"I had nothing to do with this," she said, still harboring guilt for her earlier transgressions.

Myles studied the object, taking photos and making notes. Rachel glanced at Zac, but his expression was unreadable. He exhaled sharply when Myles left the room and the screen faded to black.

Zac closed the laptop. He appeared upset, but not nearly as much as she'd expected.

"Are you okay?"

A triumphant smile flashed across his face. "Good thing I didn't leave the real one lying around."

"What was that thing?"

"A dummy, a decoy, a red herring," he said with a grin.

"What are you going to do now?"

Zac drank more wine as Rachel watched his wheels turn faster.

"I'm going to hit back, and you're going to help me. But first, I need to think." He leaned his head back on the cushion and closed his eyes.

At least she'd be playing for the right team.

Two hours later, Rachel awoke, her head on Zac's shoulder. She straightened up, and he stirred.

"Zac." She nudged his arm.

His eyes opened slowly. "Where am I?"

"You're at my place. It's late." A smile flickered across her lips. "You can stay if you like."

"Uh... yeah, okay. I'll just crash here on the sofa if that's all right."

Rachel couldn't explain the feelings that came over her. She'd feared the worst earlier, but Zac had shown compassion. She wanted to peel back the layers, as Harper must have done, to see the real man inside. Her curiosity got the best of her.

She hesitated, thinking it might be a bad idea, but she took his hand anyway. "Now, what kind of host would I be if I let you do that?"

CHAPTER 31

Zac unlocked his apartment door Saturday morning after the long walk home from Rachel's. He'd heard people speak of *the walk of shame*, but he never thought he'd be the one doing the walking. His boss at the coffee shop didn't sound happy when Zac called in sick with another lame excuse on the way home. What a schmuck he'd been. First, he lied to Rachel about Charlie, then he slept with her. What kind of man had he become?

A visit to the SPCA to find a Charlie look-alike crossed his mind. Rachel hadn't had him for long, and he wondered if she'd be able to tell the difference. Harper would. The two women were alike in so many ways that he couldn't afford to take the chance. They say the cover-up is often worse than the crime.

Zac considered another jump back to look for the dog, but he had reservations. There was no way of determining the possible detrimental physical effects from tampering with his body's energetic frequency. Was there a limit to the number of jumps that a body could tolerate? He was not about to risk losing the opportunity to save the love of his life for a dog. He would have to come clean when he showed up for work on Monday. The events of the night before would make that conversation exponentially more difficult.

His betrayal of Harper should have been tempered by the fact that she remained dead, and the probability of reversing her predicament lessened with each failed attempt. But he wasn't ready to give up. In his mind, failure was not an option.

In the light of day, Zac's plan to bait Myles with a dummy machine appeared to have backfired. He didn't know at the time that Myles had copies of his work. Although he'd disabled the decoy, someone with the information Myles now possessed might figure out what it was and how to make it work again.

Rachel switched sides. However, she hadn't earned back his trust yet. Operation Save Harper would put all of this in his rearview mirror. He didn't plan to stick around Cambridge after reuniting with Harper. He planned to move far away and never look back; a fact that he'd conveniently forgotten to mention to Silas.

The first order of business will be to design a protective cover for his wrist-mounted launch button. He'd been fortunate that Charlie hadn't started his shenanigans before he'd slipped on the backpack. There's a possibility that he could have traveled back without the TRD and been stranded in the past. A safety cover might prevent such a disaster.

After a trip to the electronics store, he spent the rest of the afternoon fabricating and installing his new cover. He worked in his apartment rather than his office or the lab for fear of running into Myles.

With nothing on his social calendar for the weekend, he needed something to keep his mind off Monday's date with destiny. He couldn't see Rachel. He couldn't even call her for fear that the conversation might circle back to Charlie. Postponing the inevitable, which was admittedly what he was doing, had won out over facing his fear head-on like a man.

Weekends have a way of moving much faster than weekdays, and this one was no exception. Likewise, his shift at the coffee shop, which sometimes dragged on Monday mornings, had somehow sprouted wings.

Zac walked into his empty office like a death-row inmate on his way to the electric chair. No more excuses. He needed to come clean about Charlie and risk destroying their complicated relationship. A soft scratching sound came from inside Rachel's bottom drawer. Zac frowned as he walked toward her desk and pulled the drawer open.

A small dog that resembled Charlie stared out at him, tail wagging.

"Charlie?"

The tail moved faster, creating a hammering sound as it bounced off the side of the drawer.

Zac's mind raced like a supercollider as he processed the scene in front of him. It can't be the same dog, can it? His brain downshifted to a more reasonable speed. While the possibility existed, finding the dog back in the drawer puzzled him.

He picked Charlie up and turned him around in his hands. He'd only spent a couple of days with him, so he couldn't tell for sure. There might be a few more gray hairs around his eyes, but he clearly reacted to the name Charlie. It took only a second for Zac to return to the present after losing him. Did this little time traveler relive the past year in the time it took to say his name?

"I have to admit, it's good to see you again." Zac turned him from side to side. "Where have you been, my little friend, and how did you get back here?"

Charlie didn't answer. His tail continued to wag.

"If only you could talk," Zac whispered. On second thought, he didn't want him sharing their little secret with Rachel.

"There you are," Rachel said from the open doorway.

Zac offered a sheepish grin.

She placed her hands on her hips. "You're lucky."

"Lucky?"

"Doctor Nelson found poor Charlie wandering around in front of the building. I thought I told you to take care of him."

The governor just called with a last-minute reprieve. "He got away from me on the way to work." He turned to Charlie. "Don't you ever run away like that again. Do you hear me?"

Zac concealed a smile as he deposited Charlie back in his drawer.

Rachel moved close, stood on tiptoes, and kissed his cheek. "Thank you."

"It was nothing." *Double schmuck.*

Chapter 32

Zac sat at his desk, puzzled over the return of his fellow time traveler. He glanced at Charlie, sitting back in his drawer, a sight he'd desperately wanted to see, but never thought possible. Disaster averted. He'd inadvertently dropped Charlie into the time stream at a point over a year ago. Their trip back there had taken only a couple of seconds. Zac returned in a similar fashion. Charlie was not so lucky. He moved with the flow like everyone else, minute by minute, hour by hour, day by day.

Charlie's year had already been lived by the time Zac returned to the present. They would sync up again, with Charlie a little worse for the wear. What Zac didn't understand was where Charlie had been and how he found his way back to campus. It didn't matter, as long as Rachel was happy. He glanced in her direction and caught a smile.

Zac dodged a bullet. He breathed a sigh of relief and refocused his energy on the project. No more distractions. He gave Rachel a list of the programmers he'd used and asked her to set up meetings to discuss further modifications.

He needed to negotiate terms to keep the cost within the limit of his remaining funds. If he explained the program's shortcomings in detail, he might get them fixed at no cost, paying only for the few additional enhancements. However, that was not an option if he continued to keep each party in the dark about the final product.

"I'm told I make a mean meatloaf," Rachel offered.

Zac said nothing. A few seconds passed.

Rachel cleared her throat. "I thought I might invite you over for dinner sometime. You know, for taking care of Charlie while I was sick."

He should have told her that such a gesture wouldn't be necessary. "Thank you. That would be nice."

"How about tomorrow night?"

He wrinkled his brow. "I'll have my assistant check my calendar."

Rachel smiled. "She says you're free."

"Then, it's a date." The words came out before he had time to think. "That came out wrong. Not a *date* date, more like..."

"A thank-you dinner?" Rachel blushed.

Zac wanted to slap on his time machine and go anywhere else. He nodded.

Rachel's apartment smelled like a five-star restaurant when Zac showed up the following evening for their *not-a-date*.

"It smells great in here. I hope you didn't go through too much trouble." He'd done nothing to deserve it.

"No trouble," she said with a dismissing wave of her hand.

Charlie watched from the sofa.

With no agenda, they settled into comfortable conversation. After one of the best meals Zac had eaten in a long time, they reclined on the sofa and listened to Bruce Springsteen. Zac became uncomfortable and withdrew.

"What's the matter?"

"Nothing."

"You don't like Springsteen?"

Zac shifted his weight on the cushion. "He was... Harper's favorite. She grew up in Asbury Park, about twenty minutes from where he was born. She listened to a lot of Springsteen growing up."

"I listened to a lot of music after my surgery. My dad bought me some nice headphones and a bunch of iTunes gift cards. I tried some of his music and liked it." She paused. "If it makes you uncomfortable, I can put something else on."

"No, I'm fine."

Zac had little experience with women, but in his opinion, Rachel Lockhart was a real catch. She appeared to like him, something she had in common with only one other woman. But a girl like Harper only comes along once in a lifetime, right? Perhaps his assumptions were flawed.

Later that evening, Zac lay in bed with his conflicted heart.

He rolled over to face Rachel. "Why did you come to Cambridge?"

"My doctor is in Boston."

He gently touched the scar on her chest. Rachel tensed and pulled away.

"I'm sorry," he said.

She relaxed. "It's okay. I don't know why I did that."

"Does it hurt?"

"Not anymore."

Zac pulled her close, and the softness and warmth of her body put him in a trance-like state until his phone rang on the nightstand. He jumped, his peaceful feeling shattered into a thousand pieces. Silas Buzzkill calling. He turned off the ringer and set the phone down.

"Who was that?" Rachel asked, her voice just above a whisper.

Zac second-guessed his decision to involve Silas and tell him the truth about his mission. He didn't have a choice, did he? However, he wasn't ready to share the details of his work with Rachel.

"It's nothing. Go back to sleep." He pulled back the covers. "I need to go."

"Wait. What's the matter?" She pushed herself up on her elbows.

"I can't sleep." He dressed quickly while she watched. "There's something I need to take care of."

"Now?"

"I'm afraid it can't wait."

"Please. Just stay. You can take care of whatever it is in the morning."

He walked around to her side of the bed and kissed her forehead. "I'm sorry."

"Jeezus, Zac!" Rachel flopped back onto the pillow.

Zac let himself out, ordered an Uber, then punched redial on his phone.

"You've been avoiding me," Silas said. "I'm glad you finally came to your senses."

Zac didn't bother to reply.

"Do you really think it's a good idea to sleep with your assistant?"

A chill crawled up Zac's back and raised the hair on his neck. He scanned the neighborhood. "Where are you?"

"I'm home in bed... where *you* should be."

"Stay out of my personal life."

"I'm afraid you don't have one of those anymore."

Zac's ride pulled up to the curb.

"I gotta go."

"Don't forget. We have a busy day tomorrow."

"Really? What are *we* doing?"

"You're picking up my daughter tomorrow, aren't you?"

He made it sound like a ride from the airport. "I can't do that yet."

"I'm getting impatient."

"It's not safe to travel. The program needs work."

"We have a deal."

"I want this as much as you. I'll check with the programmers and give you an update tomorrow."

"No more distractions."

"I'm hanging up now."

"Tick-tock, Mr. Taylor."

CHAPTER 33

Zac hadn't seen Rachel outside of work in a week. He offered a lame excuse for how he'd left the night Silas called, and their conversation had become strained. With his work nearly complete, he questioned whether he still needed an assistant, but he wasn't ready to give her up yet. He would wait for the results of the next jump.

The programmers he'd met with during the week promised to put a rush on his requests. Their finished products began arriving the previous day, and Zac spent a long night updating the TRD's firmware in his apartment. He worked from home, so he called Rachel and gave her the day off. She asked a lot of questions, and he deflected most of them.

Zac made a few tweaks of his own to the operating system and began the final preparations for what he hoped would be the successful culmination of his work. His new plan involved traveling to the parking garage beneath Harper's building and disabling her car to prevent her fateful ride. His first thought had been to unhook her battery cables, but Harper always locked her car, denying him access to the engine compartment. He needed a Plan B, so he purchased a large hunting knife to puncture one or more of her tires.

He applied the final code updates around ten in the morning. The doorbell rang as he slid the TRD into his backpack and slipped it over his shoulders. He placed the knife inside his belt, flipped up the safety cover on his wrist, and pressed the launch button. The room went black.

Pain seared the left side of his body like he'd been shot out of a cannon into a brick wall. His body recoiled, and his feet left the ground. His hand wedged awkwardly beneath him when he hit the unforgiving pavement. Blood dripped from his forehead and pooled in his eye. Blinking created a translucent pink film that made it impossible to see out of his right eye.

Zac saw the rear tire of an automobile with his good eye. A man in jeans and cowboy boots ran around the back of the car and knelt next to Zac.

"Are you all right?" He wrung his hands. "I swear I didn't see you. You came out of nowhere."

No argument there. He felt sorry for the poor bastard. Zac turned toward him, and the man's face lost its color.

"You're hurt. I'm calling 911."

Zac tried to shake his head, but the man had already dialed. His wrist exploded in pain when he moved his arm.

Zac awoke in a hospital room, tethered to an electronic monitor at the side of his bed. A clip on the end of his finger fed his vitals to the machine over a thin cable. Three walls of the tiny room weren't walls at all, but green curtains hanging from a track on the ceiling.

He had vague memories of an ambulance ride. They must have given him something for the pain.

A cervical collar held his chin high and made it difficult to see anything but the ceiling. A dull pain crawled up his right arm from a bandaged wrist. He raised the wrist in the air as high as he could. It appeared twice its normal size. He ran the fingers of his good hand over the large bandage taped to his forehead. He'd gotten himself into quite a mess this time.

The curtains parted, and a nurse stepped in. She drew the curtains back behind her, then checked the monitor and made a note on the chart in her hand.

"How are you feeling, Mr. Taylor?"

"Like I was hit by a truck."

"It was a car. In a parking garage."

Parking garage? Zac tried to sit up. "What time is it?"

The nurse stopped him and eased him back onto the pillow. "A few minutes after ten."

"PM?"

She studied him through squinted eyes. "Yes."

Zac's body went limp.

He'd made it to Harper's garage but landed in the same space occupied by a moving vehicle. Zac had become better at identifying target coordinates, but he had no way of knowing if the coordinates were otherwise occupied at the precise moment of his arrival.

"I found your ID in your wallet, but I need to verify the information."

"Where's my stuff?" Zac lifted his head off the pillow again.

She motioned toward the cabinet at the side of the bed. "Everything is right there. You need to relax."

He turned to see his wallet and a few personal items in a plastic bag on top of the cabinet.

"The police took your knife."

He didn't care about the knife. His red backpack sat on a chair next to the cabinet.

"So, your name is Zachary Taylor?"

Zac blew out a breath. "What?"

"Your name. Zachary Taylor? Like the President?"

"Yes."

"I need to verify your insurance information."

"The card's in my wallet."

"We found the card, but... there must be some mistake. It says your policy won't be issued for another six months."

"Uh... can we do this later? I'm feeling light-headed again."

"Sure. Take your time." She stood. "We just had an MVA come in, so I might be busy for a while, but I'll check back when I get a chance."

MVA. Motor Vehicle Accident? He climbed out of bed and held the curtain back a couple of inches. A doctor and three nurses occupied the room. The doctor and Zac's nurse were involved in a serious conversation. At one point, the nurse motioned in Zac's direction. He quickly drew the curtain. A few seconds later, he opened it again.

Two police officers he hadn't seen before spoke in the far corner of the room. Another sat in a chair on the other side of the curtain, most likely waiting to get Zac's side of the story. What if, in his confusion, he'd spoken to the police? What if the guard outside is waiting for him to be released so he can transport him to the psych ward? He couldn't stay there.

A curtain on the other side of the room opened, and the other two nurses he'd seen earlier wheeled a gurney from the room. A body lay still under a sheet, covered from head to toe. Harper? It had to be. There had only been one fatality that night. The other driver must be here, too. Zac wanted to find him and choke the living shit out of him, but he was in no condition.

Tears spilled down Zac's cheek. The clip pulled away from his finger when he raised his good hand to wipe them. The monitor squealed. Zac scrambled back into bed, battling pain along the way. He pulled the covers up as the nurse rushed in. The officer followed, then returned to his post, satisfied his prisoner was secure.

"What happened in here?" she asked, picking the cable up off the floor.

Zac shrugged, burrowing deeper into the mattress.

She reattached the clip to his finger, checked the monitor, then left the room.

Staying in the hospital and having to explain things to the police was not an option. He climbed out of bed, turned off the monitor, and pulled the clip from his finger with his teeth. He spit it on the floor and shuffled toward the TRD in his stocking feet and hospital gown. Unable to strap the launcher on his wrist, he held it tightly while he slipped the backpack over his shoulder.

Zac pressed the launch button and discharged himself against medical advice.

CHAPTER 34

Rachel walked Charlie along a trail near Fresh Pond Reservation. Zac had given her a few days off, so she took advantage of the mild air and sunshine to get some exercise for herself and poor Charlie. Dogs need exercise, and she'd been remiss. Charlie enjoyed the freedom, weaving his way through the grass, stopping now and then to sniff out some invisible nugget. Rachel waited patiently at each stop, using the time to figure out what Zac was up to. He'd always acted a little squirrelly, but lately, he'd outdone himself.

Their relationship had taken an unexpected turn. They'd slept together. Twice. That hadn't been the plan, but she liked how he made her feel when he was around. That is until a week ago, when he stopped coming to work and stopped answering her calls. She'd swung by his apartment to check up on him because that's what friends do. Something moved inside when she knocked on the door, but he never answered. She felt like a fool, letting herself get too involved. She hoped whatever Zac's been working on was worth it.

Rachel pulled her phone from her purse to check the time and noticed a Google alert. She stopped and tapped the link on the screen that took her to an article in the Globe about Zac. He had an accident. When? Where? The date on the article was a year old. She scratched her head as she stared at the screen. She'd been monitoring his activity. There's no way she'd missed it.

The article said little, only that he'd been hit by a car in a parking garage and suffered injuries to his head and wrist. An ambulance had taken him to Mass General for treatment.

She yanked Charlie's leash. "Come on, Charlie. We need to go."

Zac landed back in his apartment. He slipped off the backpack and set it on the table. Everything hurt. He reached for his neck with his good hand. The Velcro straps that held his collar tight let go with a tearing sound. He threw it on the floor and rubbed the back of his neck. What a disaster! Will he ever get this right? He'd come so close this time. His epic failure identified a serious challenge. The car was not something he could predict or fix with more programming.

The ends of his open gown flapped in his wake as he paced the length of the room. He removed the gown, picked up the collar, and threw them in the kitchen trash can.

Back in street clothes again, he removed the TRD from his pack and set it on the table. One side of the pack had been torn on the pavement when he fell. Everything looked intact when he examined the TRD. He would consider his landing coordinates more carefully, staying clear of places where he might end up in harm's way. If he landed in the hall outside Harper's apartment, bumping into another tenant might be the worst that could happen.

The problem with GPS coordinates is that they are only accurate to ground truth within five meters, or about fifteen feet. An intended hallway landing might put him inside a neighbor's apartment, or worse, inside Harper's apartment. Two Zac Taylors in the same room wouldn't be good for anybody. Dual-frequency receivers and/or an augmentation system would increase the accuracy. He made a mental note to look into it before the next jump.

Zac's head throbbed almost as much as his wrist. He walked into the kitchen to find some aspirin or ibuprofen. He chased down twice the recommended dose with a large glass of water. The doorbell rang, and he froze, remembering it had rung just before he left this time zone. He prayed for a Jehovah's Witness or a local politician looking for votes. He remained quiet, waiting for them to give up and move on. The bell rang again. Zac held his breath. Two rings. He hoped that was standard protocol before moving on to the next door. That's when the banging started.

"Zac? Open the door. It's Rachel." More banging. "I know you're in there."

How could she possibly know that? She was bluffing. He didn't want her to see him in his present condition. He hadn't had time to invent an excuse.

"I'm not going anywhere until you open this door. We need to talk."

Zac moved a little closer before he caved. "I don't feel well. It's probably contagious."

"I don't believe you."

Zac said nothing. A few seconds passed.

"Like it or not, I care about you. I just want to see that you're all right."

"I'm fine. I'll see you Monday on campus."

"If you don't open this door in the next thirty seconds, I'll call 911, and the police will knock it down."

He couldn't let her do that. Not after what had just happened... a year ago. He opened the door.

"Oh my God." She pushed her way into the room.

Zac's mind spun.

"What the hell happened to you?"

"It's nothing. I went out for a walk. I got carried away doing some calculations in my head and walked into the utility pole on the corner."

"Why didn't you call me?"

"Truth be told, I was embarrassed. I'll be back to normal by Monday."

"Did you go to the hospital?"

"Uh..." He shook his head while he stared at the floor. "A woman who lived in the house at the corner saw the whole thing and patched me up. I think she's a nurse."

Rachel studied him like she was deciding how much of his story to believe. "I need to go over there right now and thank her."

"Please, Rachel. That's not necessary." He motioned awkwardly toward the sofa. "Have a seat. I'll make some tea."

Zac closed the door, and she followed him into the kitchen. He filled the kettle, set it on the stove, and turned around. Rachel stood, one hand on her hip and the other holding the hospital gown and collar.

"What's this?"

He led her right to them. "Uh..." As smart as he was, he had nothing.

"You're freaking me out, Zac."

She told him about the weird alert she'd received, and how she'd gone to the hospital to see him. He wasn't there. Hadn't been there in a year. They wouldn't tell her anything more. The date of the article still bothered her.

"Your injuries are fresh, the same injuries mentioned in this article from a year ago, which, by the way, just showed up on my phone today. Why is there a gown and collar in your trash from a hospital stay that may or may not have happened a year ago? Huh? How do you explain that?"

Not in a manner that any rational person would understand. She'd backed him into a corner.

"Have I lost my mind? Gone back in time?" She threw her hands in the air. "You gotta help me out here, Zac."

He set their cups on the table. Rachel took the teapot from his shaking hand and poured.

"Thank you."

She set it on the table, then folded her arms in front of her chest and waited.

"You're going to want to sit for this," he said in a flat voice.

They sat. Rachel's gaze met his before he looked down at his cup.

"It's no secret that I've been working on a big project."

"I know. I've been typing up all your crazy notes."

Zac squeezed a shot of honey into his cup and stirred. "Not all of them."

CHAPTER 35

Rachel waited for Zac to elaborate, but he took too much time. "What's that supposed to mean?"

"It means you don't know the whole story."

"You didn't trust me?"

He shrugged. "I guess it's a good thing I didn't."

"Do you trust me now?" She reached out and touched his hand. Their eyes met.

He didn't answer right away.

She retracted her hand. "Zac?"

"Okay. I trust you."

That hurt a little. She'd been honest with him for some time now. They shared things on an intimate level. "So, what's the whole story?"

"Remember the experiment with the rat?"

"How could I forget?"

"There's something I haven't told you."

"Maybe I'm the one who should be having trust issues."

"After a couple more times with the rat..." He paused. "I tried it."

"You mean…"

"I went from my office to the one next door." He held up one hand, then the other. "One second I was here, the next I was there."

"Seriously?" She put her hand over her mouth.

"It worked. A successful teleportation."

"That's incredible, Zac."

He leaned in as if they sat in a public café, and he didn't want anyone to hear what he said next. "Something else happened. Something unexpected." He paused. "I traveled thirty feet through space, but I also traveled three minutes back in time."

"What?" The day's events made sense, if only a little. She hooked a thumb toward the device in the living room. "You're telling me that thing is a time machine?"

"I prefer the term Temporal Relocation Device."

"I don't care what you call it. If it quacks like a duck…"

"You're the only other living person who knows what I'm telling you here."

She smiled a secret smile. "What about Myles?"

"You can probably answer that better than me," he said, not hiding the sarcasm in his voice.

"I said I was sorry." Her hand trembled as she lifted her cup. She set it down. "Please, tell me more."

Zac's phone rang. He glanced at the screen.

Rachel gave him a look, and he dismissed the call.

"I've tested it a couple of times, making modifications after each test."

"I knew you were up to something." She hoped he trusted her enough to tell her. "What happened today?"

"I learned another lesson. The date on your article was accurate. You didn't see it until today because it didn't happen until today, so to speak. My jump landed me in the path of a moving vehicle.

I cut my head and sprained my wrist. After they patched me up in the hospital, I left before the police asked any questions."

"Is it okay to be walking around?"

"I'm fine. A little sore, but fine."

She held up the collar. "And this?"

"Just a precaution." He waved it off. "Now, I have a question for you. How come your phone sends you alerts about me? Are you spying on me again?"

Oops! Damage control. "I told you, I Googled you before I got hired. I guess I forgot to turn off the alerts." She snorted. "It's not like you've been blowing up my phone with all your newsworthy activity."

She needed to steer the conversation back to him. "Next time, don't go someplace so dangerous."

"Hindsight is always 20/20, isn't it?"

"You should play the lottery. You know, find out the winning number and go back a couple of days to buy a ticket. That would work, wouldn't it?"

"Yes, but it's not why I'm doing this."

"You're no fun." Her smile gave way to a serious expression. "So, why *are* you doing it?"

Zac looked for a moment like he'd swallowed his tongue. "Why does any scientist do what they do? To test theories and hypotheses about how the universe works. Scientific discoveries make the world a better place."

He had a worried look in his eyes that made her wonder if he was holding back.

"You think this time machine is going to make the world a better place?"

He didn't have an answer for that one, and his silence crawled over her skin like spiders.

Since her surgery, Rachel had noticed a heightened sensitivity to what some might call psychic energy—not quite premonitions, but an uneasy feeling or a physical sensation. She'd read about people who'd had near-death experiences and returned with supernatural powers. She did not recall such an experience, but she had existed for some time on the operating table without a heart.

She'd also read that behaviors and emotions can be acquired by the recipient from the original heart donor. Could these new feelings and sensations be Harper's? That's one of the questions she'd hoped to answer on her trip to Cambridge. Zac might offer some insight, but she couldn't straight-up ask him without giving away her secret—a secret that had become increasingly difficult to endure.

"Do you want to get some dinner?" Zac said, breaking an awkward silence.

Rachel had more questions, but she sensed the subject was closed. "Sure. You buying?"

"I guess I owe you for all the trouble I caused."

Rachel flashed a smile. "I'm just glad you're all right."

They ordered Chinese takeout and spread the cartons out on the dining room table when it arrived.

"I'm afraid I don't have any wine."

"That's okay." Rachel shook her head. "I'm trying to cut back."

"Water, it is."

Rachel placed a set of chopsticks in front of him when he returned with their drinks.

Zac held up a couple of forks. "I prefer the improved model."

"If you say so."

"What? You think I don't know how to use those things, is that it?"

"I think I'd like to see you prove it."

Zac put on a little demonstration, and Rachel nodded her approval. He explained that it was simple physics. They ate like they hadn't in days. After they'd had enough, they cleared the table and Rachel followed Zac into the kitchen. They put away the leftovers and moved back to the sofa.

Rachel sat facing him, legs folded Indian style. "Have you talked to your uncle lately?"

"I talked *about* him."

"What does that mean?"

"I got a call the other day from a rehab facility in Syracuse. They discharged him. I guess he did well, and the prognosis is good for a full recovery."

"Really? That's great."

"He's a stubborn old goat, but I've got my fingers crossed."

"I thought he said he couldn't afford rehab."

"I might have gone back to the cabin to retrieve the money he hid there."

"Seriously?"

"I had to do something."

Rachel brushed the corner of her eye with the edge of her finger before meeting his gaze. "That's just about the sweetest thing I've ever heard." She threw her arms around his neck and kissed him.

Zac's surprise didn't keep him from graciously accepting her gesture. Before long, they jumped up and left a trail of clothes into the bedroom.

CHAPTER 36

Sunlight streamed in through the open blinds. Zac had neither the time nor the money for luxuries such as curtains in his bedroom. Most nights, he'd close the blinds, but he went to bed in a bit of a hurry the night before.

The sleepover had been unexpected, so he hadn't cleaned up the place. He sat up in bed and looked around the room. In his defense, it wasn't what you'd call dorm room dirty, but vacuuming, dusting, and laundry were low on his list of priorities. He hoped Rachel was more of a big-picture kind of girl.

"You had a bad dream last night," Rachel said when she opened her eyes. "I hope it wasn't about me."

He smiled. "Not this time."

He'd had the dream again, the one where he's driving backwards and the brakes didn't work. He'd awakened terrified in the middle of the night, unsure whether he'd made any noise. Rachel stirred but never woke.

"It was nothing."

"It's never nothing. It might be a message from angels, or maybe your higher self. You need to pay attention. If you keep having the same dream, it's because you're not getting the message."

"You sound like Harper." He raised an eyebrow. "You sure you didn't know her?"

"Sometimes, I feel like I did."

He gave her a wary glance before resting his head back on the pillow. They faced each other.

"I had a dream the night I went to the hospital," she said. "I was on a beach in Costa Rica."

"Costa Rica?"

"My parents took me there when I was eleven. I fell in love with it."

"Were you a child in the dream?"

"No."

Zac waited for her to elaborate. When she didn't, he asked, "Were you alone?"

Rachel closed her eyes as if she wanted to avoid his gaze.

Again, Zac waited until the silence became awkward. "You're lucky. My dreams are not beautiful. They're frightening and make no sense."

Rachel opened her eyes, looking relieved to be off the topic of her own dreams. "You may think dreams are a bunch of random scenes that play out for no particular reason. Sometimes, they're messages."

"From my... *higher self*?"

"Fine. Believe what you want to believe."

"If that's the case, what do you think your dream meant?"

She thought for a moment. "Maybe it means I'd like to go there again someday."

"Maybe you will, but not because you dreamt about it."

"Like that's SO crazy." Rachel threw the covers back and swung her legs over the side of the bed. "Even you don't know what you don't know."

"Okay. I'm sorry." He propped himself up on his elbows. "Don't go."

"I'm not as dumb as you think. I took a course on dream interpretation in college."

"Okay. What do you think my dreams mean?"

"Well…" She sat on the edge of the bed. "Whenever you're looking or moving backward, it has something to do with the past. Driving backwards is a symbol of something wrong or dangerous. You're letting something from your past pull you in the wrong direction."

He didn't like where this was headed.

She continued. "The fact that your brakes don't work may mean you've lost control."

Ouch. He didn't think he was doing anything wrong. "You think I'm out of control?"

"I'm just telling you what I learned." Her eyes and her body language told a different story.

Zac stared at the ceiling as Rachel walked to the bathroom. She knew about his time travel, but she wasn't privy to his motivation. Had she figured it out? He'd found her, on more than one occasion, to be smarter than he'd given her credit for.

Zac berated himself for doing exactly what he'd told himself not to. He'd gotten too close. He might have to stop this from going any further. But he couldn't bring himself to do that right now, and it gave him cause for concern.

Rachel returned. "What's for breakfast?"

Zac frowned. Perhaps he'd been overthinking this.

They ate in relative silence, and Rachel disappeared right after breakfast. She made an excuse about leaving Charlie with her landlady and being eager to get back. Zac thought it may have been a reaction to their earlier conversation. He'd become far too comfortable with Rachel between the sheets. That had not been part of the plan. He needed to refocus.

Zac had been spending a little more time in front of the mirror, something nerds like himself didn't normally do. The measure of a man had always been less about what he looked like than what came out of his mouth when he opened it, or how many letters he had after his name. He considered looks superficial. What puzzled him were the women, and there'd been more than a few, that would pass up a man like himself for one with a perfectly symmetrical face and the IQ of a crayon. What was different with this one?

Zac's phone rang as he sat alone at the table, finishing the last of his cold coffee. He'd almost forgotten that he hadn't taken Silas's call the night before.

"Hello."

"When did you plan to tell me you made another trip?"

Was he following me? Eavesdropping on my conversations? Or did he find out the same way as Rachel?

"Apparently, I don't need to."

"Did you complete your mission?"

"No."

"Did the device work properly?"

"Don't you want to know how Harper was?"

It was obvious that he didn't. "Very well."

"I don't know. I didn't get to see her."

"If you're going to play games, I can send one of my people over there to help you take this a little more seriously." He paused for a moment, presumably so Zac could remember who he was talking to, or to remind him that Silas had *people*. "Tell me what happened."

"There are still a few kinks I need to work out."

"Do you need more money?"

"No."

"When do you go again?"

"When I'm ready."

The call ended abruptly. Zac set the phone down and swallowed hard. He'd had just about enough of Silas's threats. There's no way he would ever work for that man. Speaking of work, his sh*ift* at the coffee shop started three hours ago. He considered calling in sick, but it was too late for that.

Myles sat in front of one of the new Jackpot Inferno slot machines at Plainridge Park Casino, the red LED numbers representing his cash balance declining by five dollars every time he stabbed the button. The bells and whistles in the noisy room stimulated his senses, while the sirens that wailed at infrequent intervals offered hope. He needed a big win.

His phone vibrated in his pocket. He let it go, as he watched the machine swallow up more of his money. He pulled the phone from his pocket, annoyed at the interruption. A missed call from Silas. Just what he needed. He cashed out and moved to the relative silence of the lobby to return the call.

"Where were you?" Silas bellowed.

"I was busy."

"You're fired."

"What?" He spoke so loudly that heads turned.

"You heard me."

Myles lowered his voice and moved outside. "Why? Because I didn't answer the phone?"

"Because you haven't been doing your job."

"How's that?"

"I don't like hearing about what your boy Taylor is doing from other sources. I thought that's what I've been paying you to do."

Myles paced. "I don't know what you're talking about."

"Precisely my point." Silas paused. "I no longer need your services. Your first installment is due by the end of the month."

Myles removed the phone from his ear and stared at it in disbelief. He'd just blown the deal to work off his loan with Silas, and he didn't even know how. Being in debt to Silas rather than his bookie had seemed like the lesser of two evils. He would find out at the end of the month.

CHAPTER 37

Zac left his apartment in a hurry, headed for the coffee shop. The black SUV parked across the street, followed him. He turned right on Cambridge Street. The SUV did the same. Silas's *people*, no doubt. He wished he'd never asked Silas for anything. Silas needed him alive. Small consolation, but it was something. What did they want?

The SUV blocked his progress when he reached the corner of 6th and Cambridge. The door opened and two suits jumped out. Zac considered turning and running the other way, but his athletic ability was not the reason he'd been recruited by MIT. He reluctantly obliged when they ushered him into the back seat.

The driver pulled away from the curb. One of the suits produced a badge, identifying himself as an FBI agent.

"What's your relationship with Silas Gray?"

"We're not related." Zac didn't know what they knew or how they knew it, but he wasn't about to offer any information.

"You know what I meant." He frowned. "We can do this the easy way or the hard way."

"If you must know, he's the father of my dead fiancé."

"I'm sorry for your loss."

"I don't think you are."

"He paid you a sizable sum of money recently. What was it for?"

How do they know that, and why would they care? "I guess he felt sorry for me."

The agent paused, his eyes heavy with suspicion. "You can do better than that, Mr. Taylor. Easy or hard. Your choice."

Zac didn't respond.

"Let me tell you what we know. Silas Gray is a powerful and unethical businessman who has connections in the military and intelligence communities. There's been some chatter about a technological breakthrough that could be for sale. We think you might know something about it."

Unsure how to respond to the accusation, Zac said nothing.

"We're afraid it's in development and will be sold to the highest bidder. I'm sure you can understand that whatever this thing is, we must make sure it doesn't fall into the wrong hands."

The agents waited until Zac spoke.

"Look, I'm just a student. I keep to myself, mostly. I don't know what Mr. Gray may or may not be doing, nor do I care."

"I'm confused why a man like Silas Gray would write you a check for eighty thousand dollars." He shook his head. "And I'm not buying that he felt sorry for you."

"Fine. You want the truth?" Zac paused, looking him in the eye. "The money was a signing bonus to come work for him."

"What kind of work did he want you to do?"

"I'm not sure. He said he had a state-of-the-art lab where I'd work on projects that would benefit from my expertise."

"He didn't go into any more detail?"

"No."

"And that was okay with you?"

Zac turned his gaze from the agent to the window. "Where are you taking me?"

"That depends on our conversation."

"I told you everything I know," he said in a flat voice.

Over the years, Zac had become adept at burying his emotions. Inside, his stomach twisted and his adrenaline level continued to spike. On the outside, he appeared almost bored.

"You look like you got hit by a truck."

"I slipped in the shower."

"If you're smart, you won't go to work for him." He snorted. "You might *slip* again."

"Can I go now? I'm late for work."

The agent studied him through squinted eyes. He turned to the driver. "Drop him at the coffee shop."

Zac looked out the window, relieved that the car appeared to be headed for the coffee shop, but a little unsettled that they knew where he worked. How long had they been watching him? He pulled on the door handle after the car came to a stop. The door did not open.

"Not so fast."

Zac pulled the handle a couple more times.

"I'm letting you go now, but that doesn't mean we won't be having future conversations. In the meantime, don't do anything stupid."

A mixture of fear and relief washed over him. Zac said nothing, his expression intentionally unreadable.

The agent handed Zac a card. "You can reach me at that number if you think of anything else."

The doors unlocked with a loud pop, and Zac let himself out. He exhaled sharply as he watched the government-issued SUV pull away from the curb. His suspicions about Silas's motives had been confirmed. If Silas went down, the Feds would likely confiscate the TRD. Zac couldn't let that happen.

He stared at the card in his hand for a moment before slipping it into his pocket. Zac didn't know which conversation would be worse—the one he'd just finished, or the one that was about to start.

The owner of the shop stood behind the counter and gave Zac the stink eye when he walked through the door. The aroma of freshly brewed coffee masked the smell of trouble in the air. This wasn't the first time he'd been late. He didn't care for the work, but he needed the paycheck.

"Taylor. My office." His boss turned and headed toward the back of the building.

"Shut the door," he said from behind a desk when Zac entered the room.

Zac sat in the only other chair. "I'm sorry I'm late."

"You're more than late. And we both know it isn't the first time." His expression softened a little. "I enjoy helping students here, but I'm running a business."

"I know. It won't happen again."

"That's what you said the last time."

This wasn't going well, but he hoped his boss had one more chance left in him. "This time—"

"This time is different." He folded his hands on his desk. "The FBI was in here this morning asking questions about one of my employees. Not good for business. Are you in some kind of trouble?"

Zac hesitated.

"You look like you're in some kind of trouble."

"I slipped in the shower."

His boss leaned back in his chair. "I'm sorry, Taylor, but I have to let you go."

"Please..."

"I can't afford to do background checks on every employee that comes through here. I have to take people at their word. I don't know what you're hiding, but I don't need any more trouble."

"I'm not hiding anything. It was a misunderstanding."

"Even if you were a stellar employee, and you're not, I'd have to do the same thing."

Zac hung his head.

"I'm sorry, Taylor. I wish you luck in whatever you do next, but it's time we part ways. I'll put your last paycheck in the mail."

Zac stood, apologized once more, and left the building.

CHAPTER 38

For someone who hated drama, Zac Taylor swam in it. He'd dodged so many bullets lately that he'd lost count. For every step forward, he took two steps back. Losing his job yesterday meant he'd have to intensify his efforts to get Harper and get out of town.

Lines of code scrolled across his laptop screen as he looked for a way to fix what he considered still broken in the TRD program. He'd have to make the changes himself since he'd already spent the sixty grand he'd earmarked for program development. He couldn't afford to spend the additional cash from Silas on more of the same. Without a steady income, he'd have to dip into that reserve for living expenses.

Zac needed to focus. Fix the TRD and go. The programs were written in Python, a language he didn't know very well. But he was Zachary Taylor, and he was motivated. The love of his life waited for him to swoop in and save her from her unfortunate fate. The word *fate* gnawed at him.

What if fate was fate, and there was nothing anyone could do about it? What if the timeline had a way of self-correcting? What if he saved her from the accident only to lose her to something else the next day, or week, or month? Or what if the act of saving her changed the future entirely, and he returned to a present he didn't recognize, one where they couldn't be together for other reasons?

He can make the case that minor changes are like ripples in a stream. It's just random noise. Adding or removing a pebble won't affect the ripples in any discernible way. But add a big rock, and things could soon change in a noticeable way. Some things cannot be changed, while the rest of it is just noise in the time stream and won't matter.

Maybe he shouldn't try to prevent the accident at all. What if he snatched her up before the accident and brought her back with him? To the present. To where he sat right now. Drop her into the present, much like he dropped Charlie into the past. Would that somehow short circuit whatever fate may or may not have planned for her? Would it mean a second chance, a fresh start? Would the present he left behind be the same one he returned to?

His head hurt, but he needed to develop a strategy that provided the best possible outcome. Testing these theories would be time-consuming and potentially dangerous. He will have to roll the dice in real time with real-world consequences.

His big, red backpack sat on the table. He must do something about that backpack. Too easy to spot in a crowd. He needed to blend in, whether it was eluding the FBI in the present, or whatever he may have to deal with in the past. Recent events had made him feel like a fugitive, even though he'd done nothing wrong. He also wanted to reduce the size of the TRD, but any miniaturization of the components would take time and money, both of which were in short supply.

A knock on the front door startled Zac. He closed his laptop and opened the door.

"Myles? What are you doing here?"

Myles glanced up and down the street with nervous eyes. "Can I come in?"

"Sure, but—"

Myles pushed his way inside. "We need to talk."

Zac had never seen Myles like this. The man was unshakable. Today, he appeared to be anything but. He glanced at the table where Zac had been working. Zac positioned himself between Myles and the table.

Myles paced as he continued. "I'm in trouble, and I need your help."

He had a lot of nerve coming to Zac for help after spying on him and possibly undermining his project. But Myles had been a friend, as well as a professor. He'd been there for him when Zac's life and academic career fell apart. He helped him pick up the pieces when he returned to Cambridge. Zac felt obliged to at least hear him out.

"What's going on?"

"I haven't been honest with you since you've been back."

"I know." Zac didn't have the time or the patience for one of his long-winded explanations. "I have you on video going through my desk."

Myles stopped pacing and looked at Zac through squinted eyes. After a few seconds of silence, Zac urged him to continue.

"About a month after you disappeared, Silas Gray contacted me."

"Wait. Silas Gray?" The hairs on the back of Zac's neck straightened. "As in, Harper's father Silas Gray?"

"God help us if there's more than one."

Zac stared in disbelief. "What did he want?"

"At the time, I owed some not-so-patient men some money. Silas bought up my debt and offered to let me work it off."

"Doing what?"

"Finding you."

"Me? Why?"

"He didn't say." Myles shifted his weight to his other foot. "He called me the day you were arrested and told me to go down to the station and pick you up. He wasn't happy with my work up to that point."

"So, to make up for it, you set me up on campus."

"I wanted to help you get back on your feet."

"It sounds like you wanted to keep an eye on me."

"That's not the only reason I helped you. I still care about you."

"Just not enough to give me a heads up."

"My back was against the wall, Zac."

"Why are you telling me this now?"

"He sacked me. You did something recently that I was unaware of. He found out and cut me loose. On one hand, I'm relieved, but on the other, I'm scared to death. He wants me to start paying off my debt. I'm not sure how I can do that."

"What do you want from me?"

"I want you to let me help you with your project. You can have all the credit. I just want a piece of the action."

"The action?"

"Come on Zac, don't tell me you haven't thought about the commercial value of a discovery this big? And if you haven't," he said with a wry smile, "well, all the more reason you need me."

"What happened to you, Myles? We don't do these things for the money."

"Grow up, Zac. Everything we do, in one way or another, is for the money."

Zac straightened up. "I think you should go now."

Myles took a few steps and turned his head to see what was on the table behind Zac. "What are you working on?"

"I'm not kidding, Myles. You need to leave."

"Okay. I'm leaving." Myles held up his hands. "Just think about what I said."

Myles left quietly as promised, and Zac exhaled. He needed to be more careful with the TRD. Fortunately, he wasn't carrying it when the FBI picked him up. He needed a place to hide it when it wasn't with him. Zac picked up the transmitter wristband from the desk. Someone pounded on his door as he unzipped the backpack.

"Go away, Myles."

The pounding continued.

Zac opened the door. "Don't—"

A man who wasn't Myles stood in his doorway. A cigarette hung from a fat lower lip on a face that hadn't seen a razor in at least a week. He pushed one side of his leather jacket open slowly and rested his hand on the butt of a gun tucked in his belt.

"Don't what?" he asked in a low voice that sounded more like a growl.

Zac's heart moved up into his throat, making it difficult to swallow, let alone speak.

The stranger glanced up and down the street. "Can I come in?"

Assuming it was a rhetorical question, Zac stepped aside and let the man enter. He shoved the transmitter into his pocket.

"What do you want?"

The man studied the room for a moment. "Mr. Gray wants to see you."

"Why?"

He looked around the room. "Where is it?"

"I don't know what you're talking about."

"Mr. Gray told me to collect you and the machine."

Zac panicked, and he glanced at the table. Instinct told him to run toward it, but something stronger urged him to take a step back.

A stubby finger, shorter than the others, pointed to the red backpack. "Is that it?"

Zac shook his head. He couldn't let that happen. His desperation spawned an idea, and he took another step backward.

The big goon walked toward the table. Zac matched him step for step in the opposite direction. Zac crossed the invisible threshold of the transport radius as the unsuspecting goon arrived at the table. Before the goon reached for the backpack, Zac pressed the button on the wristband he'd pulled from his pocket. The goon cried out in pain.

Zac stood alone in his living room and watched a lit cigarette butt hit the floor.

CHAPTER 39

Zac crushed the cigarette out with his shoe. Only seconds before, it had been attached to a man who nearly dashed his hopes of ever seeing Harper again. Zac's quick thinking had saved him for the moment, but at what cost? He'd just sent a man back in time a full year with no way to return. Not only could there be timeline consequences, but the goon might be waiting for Zac when he returned to rescue Harper.

The pulse in Zac's neck beat double time. He pulled a chair away from the table and sat, trying to wrap his head around what he'd just done and how it might come back to bite him in the ass.

A knock at the door interrupted his thoughts. *Now what?* He hadn't heard from the FBI yet today. He didn't need any more surprises. Zac pulled himself up and walked to the window. He pushed back the curtain, something he should have done the last time. Rachel stood on his front porch with Charlie in her arms, and Zac's heart assumed a more normal rhythm. He opened the door and ushered them in.

"I'm sorry to stop by without calling, but I was afraid you'd see it was me and not pick up."

"Don't be sorry." He looked at her with forgiving eyes. She was exactly what he needed right now. "You're always welcome here."

Rachel studied him like she'd expected a cooler reception. She set Charlie down, and he went immediately to the cigarette butt. Rachel squinted to get a better look while Charlie sniffed around.

She pointed to the floor. "What's that?"

"Uh... nothing. I just forgot to clean it up."

"You don't smoke." She studied his face. "Who was here?"

"Oh, yeah." He feigned a momentary lapse of memory. "Myles stopped by."

"Professor Gordon was here?" She frowned when she said it. "He doesn't smoke, either."

"Sometimes when he's nervous..." More lies. His mind flashed back to the night before, lying in bed beside her. She wasn't the enemy, so why was it so easy to lie to her?

Charlie moved on to other parts of the room.

Rachel looked up. "What was he nervous about?"

Zac bit his tongue to keep the next lie from spewing out. He needed someone to trust. He still hoped Rachel could be that someone. Everyone he'd ever trusted had betrayed him. Maybe *he* was the problem. After all, he'd been the common denominator in every failed relationship. He'd told his share of lies.

Even Harper's death felt like a betrayal. While he'd been spending all his time and energy trying to fix that one, it seemed more and more like a fool's errand. Rachel waited patiently for his answer. He'd kept his distance from her in the beginning, something he found increasingly difficult to do as time passed. She'd hurt him like the others, but unlike Myles, her contrition came with no strings attached.

Zac opened his mouth, but nothing came out.

She took a step closer. "You can trust me, but you have to let me in. I'm trying, Zac. Can't you see..." She touched his cheek with her hand. "I love you."

"I love you, too." He said it without thinking. Was it real, or a knee-jerk reaction to the words he hadn't heard for over a year? He'd never said those words to anyone but Harper.

Their lips met, and he studied her face when they came up for air. His head told him to step away, but his heart made him stay. Her eyes held nothing but sincerity. He wasn't sure what she saw in his.

"You want the truth?" he asked.

"Always."

He led her to the sofa, and they sat. "Myles wasn't acting alone. A man named Silas Gray was behind everything."

The color drained from Rachel's face.

"Do you know him?"

"I've heard of him." She had a worried look in her eyes. "Who hasn't?"

"Myles owed him some money that he was paying off by spying on me. I haven't yet figured out why."

"Is he, I mean Silas, any relation to Harper?"

"Her father."

"So, you know him."

"I know him, but I don't like him, and the feeling is mutual." He paused. "Anyway, Silas became unhappy with Myles and fired him. Now, Myles is freaking out because he doesn't have the money to pay back the loan."

"Why didn't you two get along?"

"You mean, besides the fact that he thinks Harper's death was my fault?"

"Why does he think that?"

Zac hesitated. He wasn't ready to go there yet. "Let's just stick to Myles for now."

She nodded. "So, why did Silas hire Myles in the first place?"

A good question. Silas had hired Myles while Zac was hiding out in New York before anyone knew about the TRD. The prototype had been built at the cabin, then lost in the fire. Myles had known about his theories when he approved his dissertation request and signed on as his adviser, but Zac had been tight-lipped after that. He'd discussed the idea with Harper, but she hadn't been on speaking terms with her father.

"I haven't figured that out yet."

"If Silas didn't like you, and Harper's gone, why does he care what you do?"

"I imagine for the same reason Myles does. Money."

"What did Myles want you to do?"

"He wanted to partner with me. This thing could be worth a lot of money someday. Myles wants a cut."

"What did you tell him?"

"I told him to leave."

Her eyes drifted. "Does he know you know why he hired me?"

"Your name never came up."

She frowned. "I don't know what to do now."

"Just keep a low profile. Myles probably won't bother you anymore. My guess is he'll be on his best behavior so I'll agree to work with him."

Rachel closed her eyes and nodded, her relief palpable.

Zac debated whether or not to mention his second visitor. Rachel's respite would be short-lived. But since he had put her in harm's way, he had an obligation to warn her.

"After Myles left, I had another visitor. One of Silas's goons pushed his way in here with orders to retrieve both me and the TRD."

Rachel gripped his arm. "Oh, my God. What happened?"

Zac pried her fingers back until she let go. "I think I did something stupid, but I didn't have a choice." He took a deep breath while Rachel waited with impatient eyes. "I sent him back."

As soon as he said it, Zac knew how Silas had found out about everything.

Rachel frowned as she waited for more.

It all made sense now. His stomach bottomed out as his brain rushed to process the new information. No doubt, the reluctant time traveler reported back to his boss. What would Silas have thought about the bizarre tale of arriving from the future? It may have taken him some time to figure it out, but somehow that's exactly what he did. Zac played right into Silas's hands by going to him for money.

"You don't mean...?"

Zac nodded.

"Where did he go?"

Zac hadn't had time to set any coordinates, so Silas's goon traveled to the location of Zac's previous trip—the parking garage. Zac smiled a secret smile. With any luck, the poor bastard would be occupying a bed in the Emergency Department of Mass General when Zac returned to rescue Harper.

"Someplace where he won't be able to hurt us now."

"Jeezus, Zac. You can't start sending random people into the past."

"It's not like I planned it. I told you, I had no choice."

She grabbed his arm again. "Will he be waiting for you the next time you go?"

Zac extricated himself. "I hope not."

"Just pick a different time. Someplace where he won't be."

Zac wasn't ready to tell her why that wouldn't work for him. He may never be ready. "You're right. Easy fix."

Rachel smiled.

She wanted to help, but he couldn't tell her exactly what she was helping. Unfortunately, sins of omission are no less disgraceful.

Chapter 40

Zac took advantage of losing his job by spending the time teaching himself advanced Python programming and modifying the TRD. In hindsight, he should have done the work from the beginning, eliminating the need to involve Silas.

He'd become a pioneer of sorts, charting new courses in a field that even the best and the brightest admittedly knew little or nothing about. The goon he sent back would likely still pose a threat. He'd gone back to Harper's garage by default rather than choice. Zac knew he would turn up again, much like Charlie did. If Zac had a choice, he would have sent him somewhere into the future.

What kind of trouble might he cause by snatching Harper and depositing her in the present where, by any stretch of logic and reason, she didn't belong? It wouldn't stop him from pushing ahead with his plans. The program modifications should be completed by the middle of the week. He would have Rachel upload them to his secure cloud account for safekeeping, then attempt what he hoped would be his final rescue mission.

Zac had little time to think about what he'd do once he had Harper back, other than to live happily ever after. Staying in Cambridge was not an option. Too many threats, both physical and emotional, as well as the possibility of having to explain Harper's resurrection from the dead. They could start fresh somewhere in blissful obscurity. He'd no longer need the TRD. For the safety and sanity of mankind, it needed to be destroyed.

His life since Harper died had been a roller coaster ride. The initial drop had nearly killed him, but with the help of a friend and mentor, he climbed back up the track. From there, it had been a series of ups and downs. A new and unexpected friendship helped him through his ensuing setbacks.

Zac had to admit that he and Rachel had become more than friends. He also had to face the fact that he planned to break her heart. Why didn't he stop this relationship, whatever it was, before it started? He tried, didn't he? His whole life, he'd always been the smartest person in the room. What had gone wrong this time? He'd selfishly compromised his principles, looked the other way to ease his loneliness. He'd used her, plain and simple. The very thing she's helping him accomplish will put an end to their relationship. He wondered if they would have ended up where they were if she'd known his end game.

Zac found Rachel sitting at her desk when he arrived at the office early Monday morning. He nodded and smiled, surprised that she'd arrived before him. He stopped short when he reached his desk.

"What's this?"

Rachel's eyes lit up. "Happy birthday."

Zac frowned and scratched the side of his head. "I never told you when my birthday was."

"I Googled it."

Zac rolled his eyes. "Of course you did."

"I didn't want the day to go by unacknowledged."

He picked up the large red velvet cupcake with cream cheese frosting from his desk. His favorite. "How did...?"

She shrugged. "Lucky guess?"

Not one for public displays of emotion, Zac did his best to keep the rising tide in check.

Rachel pointed. "There's more."

Zac turned. A black Swiss Elite backpack with a big red bow sat on his chair.

"It's a new backpack," she squealed.

"I can see that." He studied the gift, turning it over in his hands.

"I think you need to be a little less conspicuous when you *travel*." She said it like it was a dirty word.

He got the feeling she didn't care much for him jumping around the timeline. Perhaps she just wanted him to be safe. The thought of replacing the backpack with a less colorful model had crossed his mind even before his red one had been damaged in the parking garage accident.

"I'm not sure what to say. That... that was really..."

"Thoughtful?"

"I was going to say unnecessary." He paused. "But your word works."

Rachel smiled.

Zac's expression turned serious, and he raised an eyebrow. "Don't you think the bow might be a bit conspicuous?"

Rachel scrunched her nose and gave a quick nod. "You might want to take that off before you use it."

They laughed.

Zac swiped at the frosting on his cupcake and licked it from his finger. The tide rose again, and he pushed it back down.

His phone rang. Saved by the bell, he thought, until he watched Silas's name scroll across the tiny screen. His face must have telegraphed his sudden anxiety as he noticed Rachel's expression fall.

"What?"

Zac ignored her. "I need to take this," he said as he scurried into the hall.

He put the phone to his ear. "What do you want?"

"How's our little project coming along? I'm anxious to see my daughter again, as you might imagine."

Zac imagined no such thing. "I told you, these things take time. I'm working on it."

Silence filled the next few seconds. "I don't like you talking to the FBI."

"It wasn't exactly my idea." *How did he know?* Zac had disposed of one of his goons, but there was no doubt more like him.

"What did you tell them?"

"Are you preparing to sell MY invention to the highest bidder?"

"Is that what they said?"

"It's not yours to sell."

"You work for me now, so technically, it is."

"Says who?"

"We made a deal. You cashed your employment advance."

"I didn't agree to anything."

"The canceled check says otherwise."

He berated himself for involving Silas. The man didn't care about anyone or anything but himself and his money. How could Harper have been this man's daughter?

"Fine. I'll give you your advance back."

"If you somehow managed to do that, and I don't think you can, we would still be partners."

The smug bastard was right. Zac let him bankroll the entire project. The money had been spent. He'd made a deal with the devil, a deal he couldn't live with anymore.

"I just need a little more time."

"You have forty-eight hours."

The call ended abruptly.

Zac paced the hall outside his office while Rachel waited, no doubt eager to hear why he bolted when the phone rang. Truth be told, she'd become almost as big a problem as Silas. He hated to admit it, but he had feelings for her. He berated himself for his carelessness. Men of science question, hypothesize, experiment, and analyze. There's no time for anything as trivial as romance.

Science had always been a way of life for Zac Taylor, with one notable exception. He'd fallen for a woman who should have shared and respected the lifestyle. But Harper Gray was different. She shared his enthusiasm for science, but had somehow been able to compartmentalize it. And while she treated it with a good deal of respect, she found a way to balance it with what some might call a richer, fuller life experience.

She'd made him soft, or perhaps deep down in places he didn't know existed, he envied her. Now, he'd fallen again one short year after Harper had left him on his own in the world. This new relationship made no sense. While the object of his affection seemed to possess a moderate amount of intelligence, she wouldn't know the difference between a particle and a wave. It didn't keep his heart from skipping a beat when she entered a room.

Zac shook his head to clear it. Even if he paid back the advance, Silas wouldn't go away. He'd made an investment that Zac had foolishly assumed was about his daughter and not about a scheme to increase his already obscene bottom line. Big mistake.

He did his best to muster a smile before returning to the office.

"Is everything okay?" Rachel asked.

"Of course." He realized he was trying too hard to conceal his anxiety, so he relaxed the muscles in his face. "I'm waiting for a call from one of the programmers. The last module is finished, and I need to go pick up a flash drive with the modified code."

Rachel studied him. "Ordinarily, I'd say that's good news, but you're acting too squirrelly, even for you." She folded her arms across her chest. "What are you not telling me?"

He didn't know where to begin. What he did know, is that he hated lying to her, but here he was doing it again. He told himself it was too late to tell the truth now. It was for her own good, anyway. Wasn't it?

CHAPTER 41

Zac left school after the call from Silas. Rachel phoned twice on his way home. In hindsight, he probably should have answered and made another of his lame excuses, but he'd grown tired of his lies. Silas had started the clock ticking, so he needed to modify his timetable. He had less than forty-eight hours to save Harper and get out of town.

Today will be the day. The TRD was as ready as it could be without another test. No time for that now. Operation Save Harper had been given the green light. T-Minus one hour and counting.

He planned to approach her after she'd left his past self in the apartment, but before she got into her car. It will appear as if Zac had run after her. However, she might question the logic, if not the plausibility, of him stopping to change his clothes somewhere in the thirty seconds it would have taken to catch up with her. Wearing the same clothes he'd worn that night provided the best chance for a smooth extraction. After a shower and a change of clothes, he'd be ready.

As quickly as the warm water relaxed the tension in his neck and shoulders, the thought of what he was about to do turned the screws and tightened everything again. This wasn't his maiden voyage. He pretty much knew what to expect, but there would no doubt be consequences when he accomplished his objective. This wasn't a pebble he planned to throw into the stream. Had he taken enough time to consider what might happen? Probably not. Science and emotion don't mix. He'd become adept at separating the two. Why was it so difficult now?

That wasn't enough, though, was it? When Zac screwed up, he did it in spades. When he'd conceived of the idea, his heart belonged to one woman, admittedly a dead woman, but a singular object of his affection. He didn't think his wounded heart had room for two, even though he now had feelings for another. He'd told Rachel he loved her. It's not a word he threw around. He would never intentionally hurt Rachel, but this was Harper Gray he was talking about.

After a long shower and a shave, Zac pulled on a pair of jeans and his MIT sweatshirt, the same one he would have been wearing had divers needed to pull him from the Charles River. He walked to the kitchen, opened the oven door, and removed the TRD from inside. He'd read somewhere that the two best places to hide something in a house were the oven and the freezer.

Zac removed the TRD from his old backpack, set the destination coordinates, and slipped it into the new one. He pulled his phone from his pocket and typed, *Goodbye, Rachel. I'm sorry, but I must go now. I'll miss you. Thank you for everything. Love, Zac.* He hit the send button and slipped the phone back into his pocket.

He strapped the launch button to his wrist and began his pre-flight checklist. All systems were go. He took a deep breath, closed his eyes, and pressed the button.

Confusion flooded his brain when he opened his eyes. He stood at the edge of the table in his living room, three feet from where he took off. Panic rose in the back of his throat. He expected to land in the hallway of Harper's apartment building approximately thirteen months ago. At that time, his apartment belonged to someone else. This appeared to be the worst malfunction yet.

He checked the coordinates. Everything looked good. He flipped up the cover on his wrist, but his finger froze a quarter of an inch above the launch button. He second-guessed giving it another try at the moment, afraid that he may find himself in a place from which it would be difficult to return, like the Charles River or the inside of a cement mixer. Travel plans had to be postponed until he could figure out why the TRD had malfunctioned so spectacularly.

Zac paced the room for an hour, going over every detail in his head. Nothing jumped out at him. He pulled a handful of programming notes from his backpack and studied each entry, but he didn't know exactly what he was looking for. He moved to the sofa and studied them until blackness, like a fog, engulfed his vision. It started at the edges and advanced inward until it filled his sight and swallowed him whole.

A knock at his door startled him, and he recoiled. He said nothing.

"Zac? Are you in there?"

"No." As soon as he said it, he regretted opening his mouth. He hadn't fully recovered from his fugue state, or maybe it was a subconscious attempt to see her one last time.

A few moments of silence followed. "Can I come in?"

He stood. "I'm busy."

"I'm worried about you."

He moved closer to the door. "You don't need to worry. I'm fine."

"Like you were fine that day on the Longfellow Bridge?"

"How do you know about that?"

"What was your last text about? Where are you going?"

"It was a mistake. Delete it."

"This is ridiculous. Let me in." She paused. "I have pizza."

Chapter 42

Zac opened the door. True to her word, Rachel held a pizza box in one hand and Charlie in the other.

"Double cheese and bacon?" He asked like it was the price of entry.

She smiled. "Is there any other kind?"

The tension slid away on their smiles, and he stepped aside. She handed him the box, still warm on the bottom. Charlie watched intently. Rachel set him down, and he followed them into the kitchen. She grabbed a couple of glasses while Zac ripped a piece of crust from the pizza and tossed it on the floor in front of Charlie.

"Who told you about the bridge?"

Rachel handed him a plate. She sat. "I'd rather not say."

Zac held the lid open while she pulled a slice from the box and deposited it on her plate. "Myles is the only person who knew about it." As soon as he said it, he remembered Myles mentioned Silas had informed him Zac was at the police station. Now it appeared we have three.

"Then I guess that's your answer," she said.

Zac watched her take a bite and chew it slowly like she was considering her next probe.

"Were you really going to go through with it?"

"You'd be surprised what people are capable of when you back them into a corner."

Rachel took another bite of pizza, and an awkward silence descended on the room. Zac helped himself to a third piece, more for something to do than to satisfy any hunger.

"So, how about those Red Sox?" he said with a smile, indicating that the previous subject was closed.

"What's the matter, Zac?"

"What do you mean?"

"You leave school in a hurry, then you send me a weird text message. So, I come over here with a peace offering because I think I did something wrong, and when I get here, you bite my head off. Good thing I brought food, otherwise, I don't think you would have let me in. Am I wrong?"

Zac shrugged.

"So, what's going on? Maybe I can help."

"You can't help." He blew out a breath. "The TRD shit the bed. It's broken, and I can't fix it."

She hesitated. "That's not such a bad thing."

"What?"

"What you're doing is dangerous."

"Walking down the street is dangerous."

"Don't be an ass. You can't compare the two."

"So now I'm an ass?"

"I thought you were working on your dissertation. Why are you even trying to build that thing?"

Zac ignored her. He took another bite of pizza.

"You've had nothing but trouble since you started this project. Maybe the universe is telling you to stop already. I think you should find another—"

"I didn't realize Myles promoted you from my assistant to my adviser."

"I never should have told you why Myles hired me."

He gave her a wary glance. Now probably wouldn't be a good time to tell her about Operation Save Harper.

"I'm beginning to think he was right. You're obviously out of control and need someone to keep an eye on you."

"Is that what you think?"

Rachel glanced at the TRD on the table. "You're obsessed with that... TURD."

"T-R-D," he corrected her.

"Whatever you call it, I'm glad it's broken."

"Don't sugarcoat your feelings."

Rachel stood.

"What are you doing?"

"You said it's broken and can't be fixed." She walked toward the table. "It's junk. I'm going to throw it out."

Zac jumped up and blocked her path. "I can't let you do that."

She attempted to push him aside. He grabbed her arms.

"Stop it. You're hurting me."

They struggled. Charlie barked.

"Let go of me," she said as she fought to free herself.

Zac pushed back harder, and she hit the floor. Charlie ran to her. She picked him up and hugged him while Zac watched.

He stood over them for a moment, taking in the insanity. What was he doing? Who had he become?

"I'm sorry," he said as he bent down to help her up.

"Don't touch me."

"I don't know what happened. I just—"

"I know what happened. I only wish I'd seen it sooner." She gained her feet. "You don't love me. You love that *thing*." She brushed herself off and exhaled sharply. "I hope the two of you are happy."

"Thank you. That makes what I'm about to say much easier."

"Really?" She put her hands on her hips. "Go ahead. Say it, Zac. You can't hurt me any more than you already have."

He took a deep breath. Perhaps it would be best for both of them. Rip the band-aid off quickly. Get it over with and move on with his plans.

"As soon as I fix that *thing*, I'm going to use it to save Harper."

Rachel's shoulders relaxed and her hands fell to her side. "What?"

"Don't make me say it again."

She bit down on her lower lip.

He'd dreaded this moment for some time. His anxiety mixed with relief.

"Has that been your plan from the start?"

Zac opened his mouth to speak, but nothing came out. He regretted the way his secret had been revealed. Part of him wanted to take it back, but it was true.

"Answer me."

"No. I started out trying to prove I could teleport from one location to another. But when I inadvertently traveled back in time, it gave me the idea that I might be able to save her."

"So you can live happily ever after? What about me?" Her tears momentarily extinguished the fire in her eyes.

Zac touched her shoulder. "I'm sorry, Rachel."

"*I'm sorry, Rachel?* That's supposed to fix this?" She slapped his hand away and huffed.

Zac recoiled, disappointed by the rebuke.

"You led me on, all the time knowing you planned to leave me. How could you?"

"I wanted to tell you, but the longer I waited, the harder—"

"I'm sorry, Zac, I don't believe you. You're getting what you've wanted all along."

Zac glared at her. He wasn't sure what he wanted.

"You don't realize what you're doing."

The tragic futility in her voice disarmed him. He said nothing as he watched Rachel and her little dog march out the door.

Zac sat at the table and stared at what was left of the pizza and Rachel's half-empty glass. His stomach twisted. He berated himself for letting his emotions take over. Part of him wanted her to throw the damn thing away. But he couldn't let that happen. Not after all he'd gone through to get here. He was too close.

CHAPTER 43

Zac awoke the next morning, feeling like he'd gone back in time. Back to the unbearable months after Harper's death. Depression weighed him down like an anchor that he couldn't drag out of bed. He felt relief once he got his secret off his chest, but he let Rachel get to him. She'd stirred up feelings of fear that he wouldn't be able to complete his mission, and guilt if he did. Fixing the TRD seemed like a no-win situation. For a moment, he considered joining Harper rather than bringing her back.

He'd been taught that if you believe it, you can achieve it. Did he still believe it? His confidence had been shaken. Perhaps all he needed was to shore up his sagging determination and press on. He wasn't ready to give up yet. He needed to focus and not let anything, or anyone, get in his way.

The broken TRD taunted him from the table when he walked by. Sitting in front of that thing all day in the stale air of his apartment wouldn't do anyone any good. He needed a different perspective, one that fresh air and a change of scenery may well provide. But first, he needed coffee. Lots of coffee.

After two cups and a quick shower, Zac stepped into the mid-morning sunshine. The smell of spring was in the air, and he breathed it in. He knew that humid air enhanced one's sense of smell. Odor molecules can pass more easily through the sensory receptors in the nose, producing stronger smells. Harper once told him that the fresh-cut-grass smell is a distress signal. A mixture of chemical defenses and first aid as the just-mowed lawn tries to save itself from the injury that had been inflicted. Distress was in the air, and it mixed with his own that lurked just below the surface.

The momentum of the confidence he mustered to get himself out of bed waned with each block he walked without a solution to his problem. He pulled out his most recent notes that he'd rolled up and shoved into his back pocket before he left the house. Studying them and paying little attention to his surroundings, he bumped into a man walking in the opposite direction. He looked up, startled to see a hairy, evolutionary misfit of a man who turned to Zac, squaring up for a fight.

"Watch where you're going, you little shit."

Zac scooped up the papers from the sidewalk. "You must be lost," he replied, in no mood for such petty distractions. "The asshole convention is two blocks *that* way."

The man's eyes narrowed. He held up a meaty fist. "How would you like a one-way ticket to the moon?"

Before Zac escalated the confrontation with another snarky remark, a firecracker went off in his brain. As unlikely as it seemed, this Neanderthal had solved the problem that had his head spinning for the last twenty-four hours.

"That won't be necessary." He held up his hands, stifling a smile. "Sorry. I'll be more careful next time." He spun on his heel and took off in the opposite direction. Zac couldn't get home fast enough.

When he turned the corner onto 7th Street, he slowed his pace. Rachel sat on his front step.

"You do realize who lives here, don't you?" he said as he approached.

"As strange as it may sound..." She forced a smile. "I'm here to see you."

It did sound strange after last night. He wasn't all that sure he wanted to see *her*. She'd nearly derailed his plans, and he didn't want to give her another chance at it.

"If I let you in, do you promise not to break anything?"

"If you promise not to hit me."

He stopped in front of her. "I didn't hit you." A whiff of lavender and vanilla made him step back. "But I'm sorry if I got a little rough."

"Can we go inside?"

Zac unlocked the door and followed her in. He glanced at the TRD on the table. Rachel noticed.

"Did you figure out a way to fix it?"

"Is that what you came over here for?"

"Yes... and no."

"Turns out it wasn't broken. The TRD uses a round-trip protocol."

"What does that mean?"

"The first push of the button takes you to the programmed destination. The second push sends you back where you came from. I designed it that way in the event of a problem that would require a quick return."

"And..."

"The last time I used it, I sent Silas's goon on a one-way trip. The next time I used it, the TRD overrode my new coordinates to complete that cycle and returned me to the take-off point of the previous trip—my living room. It did what it was supposed to do. It's not broken."

Rachel sighed. "Oh."

"I'm sorry, Rachel."

She took a deep breath and blinked a few times. "When are you going to try again?"

"Honestly?" He looked away. "If you hadn't shown up, I'd probably be gone."

"I see." She wrung her hands. "I guess I should leave."

"Wait. You said *yes and no.* What's the no?"

She took a step toward the door. "It doesn't matter now."

"Please?"

She turned to face him. "It's something I should have told you a long time ago."

"Tell me now."

A tear rolled down her cheek. "I never meant to keep it from you." She wiped the tear away and another took its place. "Well, maybe at first. It's something you need to know about me. Please don't hold it against me."

Zac sensed her growing anxiety and did his best to stay calm. He took a deep breath. Not knowing what to say, he waited for her to continue.

"Zac, just remember that I love you, and I would never intentionally hurt you." She chewed her bottom lip.

"You're scaring me, Rachel. What did you do?"

"I didn't do anything."

"I don't understand."

She stared at the floor. "It involves Harper."

"What? My Harper?" He frowned. "You knew Harper?"

"I never actually met her, but—"

"Rachel. What is it?"

She met his gaze. "I have her heart."

"What?"

"My heart transplant. The donor was a woman named Harper Gray. It meant nothing to me at the time."

Her words landed like a knee to the groin. "No. That's not possible. Tell me you're kidding. Tell me this is some kind of cruel joke. Please. I'll forgive you, but please tell me you're not serious."

"It happened a little over a year ago. I needed a heart, and there was a car accident. I'm sorry, Zac."

A sharp pain snaked its way between his eyes and coiled up at the base of his brain. He squeezed the back of his neck. Did she just apologize for receiving an organ donation that saved her life?

"Say something."

He couldn't speak if he wanted to. Frankly, he didn't want to. He wanted her to take it back. He wanted it to be a joke, a dream, a mistake. Anything but the truth.

"Is this a ruse to get back at me? To keep me from going?"

"It's the truth. I wish it wasn't, but it is."

"What are you saying?"

She paused, and her eyes pleaded with him. "You can't go."

Zac shook his head slowly. "You don't understand..."

"I understand that I've been a fool. The whole time I've been helping you destroy me."

"You're saying if I go back and save Harper..." His words trailed off.

"You can't even say it, can you?"

He hesitated. "I thought if I didn't say it out loud, maybe it wouldn't be true."

Rachel's tears flowed freely.

He wanted to hold her in his arms and tell her everything would be all right. But that would be a lie. He'd lied enough.

Zac did nothing. Absolutely nothing.

"If you do this... I'm going to die."

A thousand spiders crawled up Zac's back and down his arms. He stared into the abyss, the dark side of playing God. It had been an easy decision to this point, giving life rather than taking it. He'd made his peace with playing God. Playing the grim reaper took it to a whole new level that he was ill-equipped to handle.

Zac grasped at straws. "You don't know that's going to happen."

"You don't know that it won't."

He didn't. Not for sure. There was a lot he didn't know.

"I know two people can't physically share one heart," she continued. "If she doesn't die, I lose my one chance to live."

"Maybe another heart would come along."

They both knew it would be a long shot. He saw it in her eyes.

"You need to let her go."

She may be right, but he wasn't ready to do that. He found it difficult to breathe. The room spun, and he had to sit.

Rachel waited for a response that didn't come. "The past is the past for a reason. If it should have, it would have."

"Maybe the past got it wrong."

She threw her hands in the air. "You have an answer for everything, don't you?"

He pulled himself up.

"You told me you loved me."

He swallowed hard. "I do."

She took a step closer and slapped his face. "You're a liar."

He watched her slam the door on her way out.

Chapter 44

How did this happen? He had to fall in love with the one woman on the planet who'd received Harper's heart. No doubt the reason he fell for her. In hindsight, she said and did a lot of things that reminded him of Harper. That's crazy, right? She didn't get her brain. It was an organ—eleven ounces of muscle and tissue. Simple biology. He sat at the table in front of the device that would most likely put an end to Rachel's life. A device he created. He rested his head on folded arms and cried.

Eventually, he raised his head and wiped the tears from the table with his sleeve. A fierce debate raged in his mind. He tried to shut it down, replace the thoughts with something else. Nothing worked. He'd been captain of the debate team in high school. He knew how to craft an argument for one side of an issue, but he played for both teams this time.

He'd only known Rachel for a short time. True, but if a gunman killed a perfect stranger, it wouldn't be any less wrong than if he killed a friend. On and on he went, arguing brilliantly for both sides.

He had an impossible decision to make. He'd loved two women in his life. It was the first time he'd admitted it, but it was true. Now he must choose which one lives and which one dies, something he wouldn't have to consider if he hadn't stumbled on time travel in his experiments. Playing God was not something he cared to do.

Zac's phone rang. Myles calling. He let it go to voice mail.

The FBI appeared to have him under surveillance. Silas's deadline loomed, and he couldn't be sure what the man was capable of doing if it passed. Now, a desperate Myles wanted to meddle in his work. Circumstances that he created had thrown him into a pressure cooker.

Suddenly, as if a switch had been thrown, his brain went on autopilot. He'd taught himself this technique when he needed to stop overthinking and follow the plan he'd put into place. He walked into the bathroom, threw cold water on his face, and ran his wet fingers back through his hair. Then he changed into the clothes he'd worn that night one year ago and sat down in front of the TRD. With the launch button strapped to his wrist, he began the preflight check.

All systems go. Don't think, just do. He pressed the launch button, unaware that Rachel watched through the front window.

Zac opened his eyes to find green commercial carpet and beige walls with brass sconces. A perfect landing. Fifteen feet down the hall, he found the door to apartment 2B—Harper's apartment. He checked his phone. 9:11. Harper would storm out that door in about ten minutes unless he did something to stop her. Zac had been so preoccupied with getting there, he hadn't given much thought to what he would do when he arrived.

Making it there safely was all that mattered at the moment. He'd figure out the rest as he went along. He'd figure out the rest along the way. One of him was already inside her apartment. What would happen if they met? How would Harper react upon seeing both of them? He didn't remember seeing himself that night in her apartment a year ago.

There were no written rules, no time travel handbook to consult. All anyone could do was speculate. He had to bring her back. That part he knew. While it seemed like his only option, he didn't know the potential consequences. Would she have simply disappeared a year ago with no explanation, no goodbyes? What would his life have been like for the past year? What would it be like when he gets back?

Zac had more experience than anyone, but it was limited. He'd been careful not to change things in his travels for fear of future timeline consequences. The recent revelation about Rachel's heart transplant complicated matters exponentially. He'd left Charlie behind on one of his trips, and the dog still ended up back with Rachel one year later. But what he was about to do here could have far more dire consequences. How could he be sure of anything? His stomach rolled and his head pounded. He steadied himself against the wall.

Angry voices echoed from inside Apartment 2B. He took a couple of steps closer.

"You're a big girl, Harper," he heard himself say. "Your father has no right to tell you who you can or can't marry."

"That's not the way he sees it."

"Then you need to tell him... or I will."

"Yeah, like that's a good idea. You'd just make things a thousand times worse."

"Why do you put up with his shit?"

"Why do you think?"

"You don't need his money."

"Really, Zac? What planet are you living on?"

"Look at us. We're intelligent people. We're going to be successful at whatever we do."

"Well, when that day comes—"

"I don't want to wait."

"You think I do?" Her voice cracked.

"Then talk to him."

After a few seconds of silence, he raised his voice. "Dammit, Harper. Don't push me away like this. I thought we wanted the same things."

Harper's phone rang.

Out in the hall, Zac frowned. He didn't remember her getting a phone call.

Back inside the apartment, the altercation continued.

"Was that him?"

"I have to go."

"Where?"

"I'd rather not say."

"He says jump, and you ask *how high*. Every single time."

"That's not fair."

"I'll tell you what's not fair—"

"You probably shouldn't be here when I get back."

"Don't go."

"Goodbye, Zac."

"I'm going with you."

"No, you're not."

Zac mustered enough strength to backpedal around the corner out of sight. He leaned his head back against the wall. It wasn't his fault. Why didn't he remember that? She got a phone call from her father. That's why she ran out of there. The guilt had been such a large part of his life for the past year; it proved difficult to let go. He should have said something more to stop her. It was a feeble attempt to hold on to his guilt, and he knew it. Harper was as stubborn as she was beautiful.

The door opened, and he peered around the corner. His heart stopped momentarily when Harper stepped into the hall. He'd underestimated the emotional impact of seeing her in the flesh again after more than a year. He wanted to stop her, wrap his arms around her, and never let go.

Instead, he watched her slam the door and march down the hall toward the elevator. He'd have to grab her in the parking garage before she reached her car. He would tell her the truth if he had to.

What about Silas's goon? Was he there yet? Would he become a problem? Zac smiled when he realized the parking garage accident would be the perfect cover. No one would pay attention to the two of them when they vanish into thin air.

He wiped the sweat from his palms when the elevator doors closed and hurried toward the stairs.

CHAPTER 45

Rachel stared through the window at the empty chair where Zac had been sitting only a few seconds ago. A small part of her thought he might change his mind. He'd told her he loved her, and she hoped he would prove it by leaving the past alone. She trembled as the larger reality sank in—she was about to die.

She didn't know how much time she had. They might return at any moment, ending her life right there on his porch. There were things to do before... she couldn't bring herself to say it out loud. Zac's words from a few hours ago echoed in her head. *I thought if I didn't say it out loud, maybe it wouldn't be true.*

Unfortunately, that was a load of crap. She loved Zac, but he didn't feel the same way about her. The empty chair was proof. She ran down the stairs to her car. Ten minutes later, she sat in her parked car in front of her apartment. She pulled her phone from her purse and dialed.

"Hi, Mom."

"Rachel. It's so nice to hear your voice."

"I'm sorry I haven't called in a while, but I've been pretty busy."

"That's okay, honey. Did you find the information you were looking for?"

Rachel hesitated. "Yeah, Mom." She wiped a tear. "I guess I did."

"Will you be coming home soon?"

"It looks that way." More tears. "I love you. Tell Dad the same."

"We love you too, dear."

An awkward silence interrupted the conversation.

"Are you all right?"

"I'm fine. I'll see you soon." She ended the call seconds before she burst into tears.

In a short time from now, they won't remember her call. It will have never happened. All they will have will be the memory of burying their daughter months ago.

She ran up the stairs and into her apartment, deciding what she needed to do in the time she had left. Charlie greeted her with his usual enthusiasm.

"Charlie." Tears fell again, and whatever else she might need to do didn't matter. "What am I going to do with you?"

She picked him up and squeezed him. "Who will look after you?"

He licked the side of her face.

She pulled out her phone, wiped the tears on her sleeve, and dialed Zac's number, not expecting him to answer. She hoped he wouldn't. He'd get her message when he returned.

"I guess this is it," she said into the phone. "I loved you, Zac. I wish you chose me." Her voice cracked, and she hesitated. "I have one last favor to ask. Please take care of Charlie for me."

After a long moment of silence, she whispered, "Goodbye, Zac."

She put a few of Zac's things that he'd left at her apartment into an overnight bag. She put all the cash she had in an envelope and placed it in the bag with her laptop and her journals, then slung the bag over her shoulder. After gathering up Charlie's food and his water bowl, she picked up the end of his leash and left the apartment without looking back.

She drove quickly to Zac's place, afraid she might vanish and leave Charlie alone in a moving vehicle without a driver. Bittersweet memories filled her head as she stared at the front of Zac's apartment from her parked car.

"Come on, Charlie. This is your new home." She grabbed everything and left her car. Dead woman walking. She set everything down on the front porch. The laptop in the bottom of the bag made a thud when it hit the floor. No worries. She was still alive, so clearly Zac had not returned yet.

She sat next to her dog. "I'm going to miss you, Charlie."

He looked up at her with sad eyes.

"You're going to stay here with Zac and..." She paused. "I need you to be a good boy."

She looked back at the past year, a year that had been a gift. She had mixed feelings about how she had spent her time. What if she never came to Cambridge? It probably wouldn't have changed her fate. Zac would have invented his time machine and saved Harper. At least this way, she saw it coming. She wiped the tears that rolled down her cheeks. As foolish as it sounds, she treasured the time she spent with Zac. She wouldn't have changed any of it.

A sound startled her from behind. She turned to find Zac standing in the open doorway. She gained her feet quickly. Her jaw followed a second or two behind. They locked eyes.

"You're back." Rachel glanced down and scanned her body. "I'm still here. I don't understand."

Zac smiled. "A good friend of mine once told me, 'The past is the past for a reason. If it should have, it would have.'"

"You mean...?"

Zac nodded.

Rachel stared, unable to speak. Tears flowed, and she wiped them away with both hands.

"I chose you, Rachel."

He stepped out onto the porch. Rachel hurried to meet him. Their lips locked in a kiss that stood the test of time. Charlie barked his approval.

Rachel studied his eyes when they came up for air. "Why?" She smiled. "I mean, I'm thrilled, but you were dead set on going back to save her. I never imagined we'd be standing here like this."

"I wish I could say it was love at first sight. We got off to a rough start, and that's on me."

"Actually, it's not. I may have been stalking you a little. I wanted to die that day you caught me on your porch. Then Myles threw me at you. It was obvious you didn't want an assistant."

"If it's any consolation, after I got a look at you, I told Myles if I must have an assistant, I wanted someone who wasn't so pretty. I didn't need any distractions."

"I'll take that as a compliment." She blushed. "So... was I a distraction?"

"You could say that." He gave her a wink. "Let's go inside."

They gathered Rachel's things and the three of them stepped inside. Rachel followed Zac into the kitchen, where he set the bag of dog food on the floor. Rachel dropped her bag in the corner and handed him Charlie's bowls.

"Looks like someone's planning to move in."

Rachel shrugged. "I didn't know what else to do with him."

"What about you?"

"What do you mean?"

"Maybe you can join us."

Her eyes grew wide. "Move in here?"

"Why not?"

She hesitated, and his heart sank.

He took her hand, and they sat on the sofa. "I know I've been acting like a crazy person. I've been dealing with some things that..."

Rachel waited for him to continue.

"Ever since the accident, I struggled with the feeling that her death was my fault. That guilt nearly destroyed me, and in the end, I took it out on you. I hope you can forgive me."

She nodded.

"When I went back, I realized it wasn't my fault, and her accident is why you're here. It all happened for a reason, and I needed to accept that and leave it alone. If it should have, it would have. That's what you said. And you were right."

"I truly believe that, and not just because of my situation." She sighed. "I'm grateful that you do, too."

Zac leaned in for a kiss. Rachel threw her arms around his neck. Charlie barked, and they stopped to laugh.

"I think he's going to like it here," Rachel said.

Charlie's bark turned into a low growl, and Zac frowned. He walked to the window and pulled the curtain back enough to peek outside, then quickly let go. Silas's goon, the one with the sawed-off finger, the one who Zac had sent into the past, was back and marching up the walk toward his front door.

CHAPTER 46

Zac turned to Rachel. He pointed at Charlie and held his finger to his lips. Rachel picked him up. Zac watched the goon pull a gun from his belt just before the curtain fell back into place. The big, angry son-of-a-bitch had an ax to grind with Zac, not Rachel. He needed to get her out of sight and keep Charlie quiet. Zac glanced at the front door. He hadn't locked it after they came inside. No time to lock it now.

Zac ushered them both into the bedroom closet.

"What about you?" Rachel asked with panic in her voice.

"I'll be right out here. He wants me. If he finds me here, he probably won't go looking any further."

"You can't do that. I—"

"It's not up for debate."

She glared for a moment. "Be careful, Zac."

Zac opened the bedroom door a crack. The goon stood in the living room, his gun drawn. He stared at the TRD on the table. Zac berated himself for not grabbing it before they retreated to the bedroom. He wondered if the goon was having second thoughts about touching it after the last time. He walked toward the kitchen before Zac closed the door.

The door wouldn't lock from the inside. Someone had installed the hardware backwards prior to his moving in. Zac could have fixed it himself with nothing more than a screwdriver, but he never took the time. Rather, he'd slept with the door open for fear of inadvertently locking himself in. It may have been a fatal mistake. He grabbed a chair and wedged it underneath the doorknob.

Zac sat on the end of the bed and waited, ready to give himself up to save Rachel... again. The floor creaked outside the bedroom door. He held his breath. The doorknob turned, but the chair held. He prayed that the sound wouldn't set Charlie off again. Another push, harder this time. The next few seconds felt like an hour. The floor creaked, followed by footsteps moving away. Zac removed the chair and eased the door open a crack. Silas's goon disappeared out the front door with the TRD under his arm.

"He's gone. You can come out now," Zac said.

The closet door remained closed.

Zac opened the door to find Rachel crying. "I said, he's gone."

"I didn't know whether he forced you to say that to keep him from putting a bullet through the door. I don't want to die."

"You're not going to die." He wrapped his arms around her. "We're safe. I watched him leave."

"Thank you for—"

"He took the TRD."

"That's okay. You don't need it anymore."

"It's *not* okay!"

"Why? You're not going back again. Please tell me you haven't changed your mind."

Zac didn't hear her. His mind was too busy running through a frightening list of possible scenarios where Silas controlled the TRD.

"Well...?"

"No. I haven't changed my mind."

She shook her head slowly. "It's like you have a get out of jail free card. All you need to do is push a button, and I'm out of your life for good. And it's not like you'd even miss me. You'd have Harper."

"Don't be silly. That's not going to happen." He ran his hand back through his hair. "It's not so much that I want the machine, as I don't want Silas, or anyone else, to have it. It's way too dangerous."

"He doesn't know how to use it."

"If he threw enough money around, he'd find someone to figure it out. Hell, Myles would find a way to do it if it meant getting out from under his debt."

"Sounds like we need to get it back."

"Not we. Me."

"If you think I'm going to let you go over there alone..."

"This is my fight. I'm not going to drag you into it."

"This is *our* fight now."

"I appreciate the sentiment, but I have to do this alone."

Rachel put her hands on her hips. "And how are you planning to get across town?"

"I'll order an Uber."

"Really? You think that driver's gonna have your back if things go sideways?"

Zac frowned as he considered his reply. "I guess I could use a wheelman." He sighed. "But you're staying in the car."

They said goodbye to Charlie, locked him in the bedroom, and left in Rachel's car.

"What's the plan?" Rachel asked.

"Get the TRD back."

"Why didn't I think of that?" She offered a sarcastic smile.

"I don't have a plan at the moment." He stared into the side mirror. "I was hoping something would come to me on the way there."

"What if it doesn't?"

"Turn here," he said abruptly.

"What?"

"Turn!"

Rachel turned the wheel hard. The tires squealed as the car careened around the corner. "Where are we going?"

Zac looked out the back window. The black SUV he'd been watching in the mirror made the same turn. "I think we're being followed."

"What? Who would be following us?"

"I'm not sure." He *was* sure—a government-issue black SUV like the one he'd ridden in a few days ago.

"What do we do now?"

Red lights flashed on a railroad crossing ahead. "Step on it."

Rachel stepped on the accelerator, then backed off. "There's a train up ahead."

"I know."

"The gate's coming down."

Lights on the gate flashed their warning. "Just do it."

"But Zac..."

He unbuckled his belt, reached his leg across the seat, and stepped on the gas pedal. Rachel screamed, her foot trapped beneath his. She closed her eyes.

"Drive, Rachel!"

The train, fifty feet away now, blasted an urgent warning. Rachel screamed. They cleared the tracks with a half-second to spare.

On the other side, Zac turned around. Nothing but train. "Yeah!" He punched the air with his fist as he pictured the SUV stuck behind the gate, the driver pounding the steering wheel.

Rachel let go of the breath she'd been holding as their car came to a stop. "What just happened?"

Zac smiled briefly. "We lost the tail."

No time to celebrate one small victory. We must stop Silas before he does something stupid like try to use the TRD himself.

"The good news is we lost them for now."

"What's the bad news?"

"They might have another car waiting around the next corner."

"Let's do this." Rachel stepped hard on the gas, leaving a small patch of rubber behind.

A block from Silas's mansion, Zac instructed her to pull over.

Rachel obliged. "What are we doing?"

"I want him to think I came alone."

"How do you propose we do that?"

"I need to drive."

"You don't drive."

"How hard can it be?"

"Have you ever driven before?"

"Get in the back and stay down."

Zac guided the car down the street a little below the speed limit, pulled up to the big iron gate, and rolled down the window. A voice crackled from the intercom speaker.

"I've been expecting you."

Zac glanced up at the camera perched atop one of the massive stone columns. "You have something of mine."

The gate opened, and he drove through. He parked along the large, circular drive, far enough from the house that the door cameras might have a difficult time detecting any movement inside the car.

"I'm going in. You stay put."

"Back here?"

"Don't leave the car."

"What am I, five years old?"

Zac took a deep breath and walked up toward the house. The front door opened, and he disappeared inside.

CHAPTER 47

Rachel watched from the back seat as the massive building swallowed Zac whole. She climbed into the driver's seat. Her fingers tapped the steering wheel while she waited. *What's going on in there?* She checked the time. Five minutes seemed like a half-hour. There must be something else she could do.

She watched a UPS delivery truck pull through the gate and drive toward the back of the building. Rachel started her car and followed. The truck stopped near a door marked *deliveries*. The driver jumped down, propped open the marked door, then opened the back of the truck. He offloaded several boxes onto a handcart and wheeled them inside. Rachel hurried toward the truck.

She leaned inside the driver's door and grabbed a brown UPS cap and a couple of pieces of paper from the floor. Her cover would be blown if she ran into the real driver inside, but it might buy her some time with the hired help. Rachel noticed a camera above the door, so she slipped the cap on and strolled into the lion's den.

The room, which appeared to be a small office, was empty. A steaming cup of coffee sat atop a stack of papers on the desk. An adjoining room contained a bank of video monitors displaying various parts of the property. Voices echoed from inside.

A hallway led to another part of the house, and she followed it. It turned into a maze of doors and more hallways. She turned a corner and came face to face with a stocky man with enormous arms and a five o'clock shadow.

One look told her he was the kind of person you go out of your way to stay out of his. That wasn't an option now.

He pointed a sawed-off finger at her. "What are you doing here?"

Unsure whether he was smart enough to read the letters on her cap, she said, "I have a delivery."

He looked at the papers in her hand. "Where is it?"

He was smarter than he looked. "Uh... it's in the truck. It's a large box, and I didn't want to bring it in until I found someone to sign for it." Not bad, she thought, proud of her quick thinking.

"The delivery truck left two minutes ago."

She panicked but made a quick recovery. "*Dammit.* I told him to wait until I got back." She flashed a nervous smile. "You know how it is when you're training someone new."

The big goon hesitated.

"I need to use your phone."

He studied her for a moment, and she thought she'd pulled it off until he lunged for her. Rachel ducked out of the way. She attempted to get around him, but he hooked her leg with his massive foot and sent her to the floor. He looked at least ten feet tall from down there.

Zac's escort, one of Silas's goons with all his fingers, ushered him into Silas's office. The TRD sat on a large mahogany table. Silas studied the launch controller, turning it in his hand.

"You had no right stealing that."

Silas set the controller down. "It appears we have a difference of opinion."

"You said I had forty-eight hours."

"Did I say forty-eight?" He smirked. "I meant twenty-four."

The muscles in Zac's neck tightened and his head throbbed. "You can go to hell."

This appeared to amuse Silas, but only for a moment. "I have something important to do and you're going to provide the transportation."

"Don't you have a chauffeur?"

"Yes. But we're not traveling by car."

"If you think—"

"Please don't interrupt." He continued, gesturing toward the table. "We're going for a ride in your little time machine."

"Over my dead body."

"I'm afraid that can be arranged."

A noise from outside the closed door interrupted their conversation. A few seconds later, the door swung open. Silas's time-traveling goon filled the doorway. He stepped into the room with a kicking and struggling Rachel in tow.

Silas gave two quick claps of his hands like he was addressing his pet Rottweiler. "Rocco. Please. That's no way to treat our guest."

"I found her wandering the halls." He let go of Rachel and shook his right hand in the air. "She bit me."

Zac glanced at her UPS hat and gave her an *I-told-you-to-stay-in-the-car* glare.

"This just got interesting." A diabolical smile crossed Silas's face. "We could do this over Miss Lockhart's dead body."

Zac watched the color drain from Rachel's face.

"Now then," he held up the launch bracelet. "How does this thing work?"

Zac grabbed it from his hand. "Depends on what you had in mind."

Rachel's eyes widened. "You're not seriously considering—"

"Rachel. Please. Let me handle this." Zac strapped the launcher to his wrist. He had an idea, but it required timing and a little misdirection.

"You realize that wherever we go, you can't change anything. There could be serious consequences."

Silas shook his head. "And this from a man who plans to raise someone from the dead. I suggest those consequences would be far more serious." He turned to Rachel. "How do *you* feel about all that?"

Rachel said nothing.

"Where are we going?" Zac said after an awkward silence.

"That's better." The muscles in his face relaxed as a small, triumphant smile flashed across his lips. "Our destination is 2015. The morning of September third, to be exact. At a little after ten, I walked away from a deal that would have made me tens of millions of dollars and crushed one of my fiercest competitors."

Zac wondered how much of this recent turn of events was premeditated. Did Silas even care if Harper returned from the grave, or was it simply a means to use Zac's technology for his own selfish ends? He'd been a fool to believe the former.

"I don't think this is a good idea."

"Frankly, I don't care what you think."

Silas opened a drawer, pulled out a gun, and placed it on the desk in front of him. "Are we going to do this or not?"

"How do I know you won't kill her when we get back?"

"You don't."

Zac folded his arms defiantly.

Silas set his hand on the gun. "If you don't take me where I want to go, you can be sure that I will."

Chapter 48

Rachel stood too close to the TRD for Zac's plan to work. He motioned subtly for her to back up. She watched with a confused expression. Zac took a step backward, then nodded to Rachel with raised eyebrows. Rachel telegraphed her recognition. She took a step back, but Rocco grabbed her arm and pulled her forward.

Plan B. Zac slid the TRD to the other end of the table.

"What are you doing?"

"Better light over here."

Zac glanced at Rachel, calculating her distance from the TRD's new location. He nodded.

Silas watched as Zac began setting the coordinates.

"September third, you said?"

Silas gave a nod. "Yes. 2015. Sometime before 10 am." He tapped his fingers on the table as Zac worked over the device. "How do I know you'll take me where I need to go?"

"You don't."

Silas picked up the gun and moved closer. "Let's go, so I can fix this thing once and for all."

Zac turned and took a couple of steps.

"Where are you going?"

"Nowhere. I need a moment."

The metallic sound of a bullet entering the chamber of Silas's gun froze Zac in his tracks.

"I'm getting impatient."

Zac stopped four feet from the table. He needed to put another two feet between himself and the TRD, or he would accompany Silas. He turned around and held up his hands. "I need to think. I'm not accustomed to this kind of pressure."

He paced in a tight rectangle, aware that the business end of Silas's gun followed him like he was a tin duck in a carnival shooting gallery.

"We don't want to get this wrong," he added, hoping that talking might distract Silas enough that he wouldn't notice Zac's pacing took him farther away from the table. He couldn't keep it up much longer without Silas suspecting something. He estimated his distance to be about six feet, right at the edge of the transport radius.

Silas turned the gun on Rachel. "You won't like how this ends if you make me wait much longer."

"Just a few more seconds."

The sound of an explosion echoed from every corner of the room. It took a second to realize that Silas had pulled the trigger. Zac spun around to find Rachel on her feet. Silas glared, his hand in the air and a fresh bullet hole in the ceiling. Zac exhaled sharply.

Silas brought the gun down and pointed it again at Rachel's head. Zac's eyes followed. Rachel's bottom lip trembled.

Zac raised his arms. "I figured it out."

Silas relaxed, and Zac slowly brought his arms down. "All this time, I thought it was my fault, but *you* killed her. You and your selfish, misguided—"

"What are you talking about?"

"You need to fix something?" He locked eyes with Silas. "Fix this!" Zac stabbed the transport button.

Silas disappeared.

An eerie silence descended upon the room.

Zac turned to Rocco. "You want to be next?"

The big goon took a step backward and hesitated for a moment before placing his hand on his gun. He clearly didn't have two brain cells to rub together, but his eyes told Zac that the one he had remembered how he took a similar trip. He couldn't get out of the room fast enough.

Rachel turned to Zac. "I can't believe you just did that."

"What choice did I have?"

Her face tightened, and she bit down on her lower lip.

"He can't hurt us, at least not for a while?"

"You heard him. He'll change things that could have consequences for a lot of people, including us."

"That's not going to happen."

"How can you be so sure?"

Zac smiled. "I sent him three months into the future."

Rachel frowned. "I didn't know you could do that."

"Neither did I."

Zac never had a reason to travel to the future, so he hadn't tested it. He didn't know if it would work, but in that moment, he hadn't had time to think. Three months will allow him time to figure out how to avoid Silas when they sync up again.

"We need to put Cambridge in our rearview mirror before we catch up to him."

Rachel blew out a breath. "You won't get any objections from me."

"Right now, we need to get out of here." He packed up the TRD and slung the backpack over his shoulder.

"My car is around back."

"Do you remember how to get there?"

The door to Silas's office burst open, and two men rushed in like Starsky and Hutch, guns and badges held high.

"FBI," one of them shouted. "Put your hands where we can see them."

CHAPTER 49

Zac stared at the business end of a .45 caliber pistol, aware that a similar piece was pointed at Rachel. They both raised their hands.

"Where's Silas Gray?" one agent asked.

Zac recognized him as the agent who questioned him in the car. He shrugged. "He's not here."

"I can see that." They dropped their badges but kept their guns aimed. "What are you doing in here?"

Zac hesitated. "Mr. Gray called and said he wanted to meet, but he never showed."

The agent looked Rachel up and down, stopping at her hat. "Who's this?"

"A friend."

Starsky and Hutch turned to each other but said nothing.

"How did you get in here?"

"The butler let us in."

Starsky looked from Zac to Rachel, then back to Zac. "Let's all go for a ride."

"I have a car." Rachel offered. "I can drive him home."

Hutch patted Rachel down, then did the same to Zac. "Neither of you is going home anytime soon."

"Are you arresting us?"

Starsky holstered his pistol. "We need to ask you a few questions."

"What's in the backpack?" Hutch asked.

"My computer."

"You always carry a computer with you?"

"I'm a physicist. My computer is the only one who understands me."

He held out his hand. "Let's see it."

Zac slipped it off and handed it to Hutch, who unzipped it and folded back the flap. Zac held his breath while the agent studied it. He poked at it a couple of times, then nodded to his partner.

Zac resumed breathing and returned the pack to his shoulder.

Hutch left the room to search the rest of the house while Starsky kept an eye on the prisoners.

"So, you said Silas called you?"

Zac nodded.

"Any idea what he wanted?"

"Nope."

"What is your relationship with Mr. Gray?"

Zac tried to remember what he'd told him the last time. "He would have been my father-in-law, but my fiancé died in a car accident."

Starsky nodded.

Zac glanced at Rachel, who stared at the floor. He said nothing.

"So, this was a personal visit?"

"I can't imagine what else it would have been."

"He gave you a large sum of money recently. You told me it was for..." He pulled a small notebook from his shirt pocket and flipped through the pages. "Here it is... a signing bonus to work for him." He pocketed the notebook and looked up at Zac. "That doesn't sound personal to me. You sure it didn't have anything to do with that?"

Zac caught Rachel's glare in his peripheral vision. "I told you, I don't know what he wanted."

The agent turned to Rachel. "Is there something you'd like to say, Miss..."

"Lockhart. No."

Hutch returned, looked at his partner, and shook his head.

"Okay. We need to finish this downtown."

The agents led Rachel and Zac through the house and out the front door. Silas's two goons had made themselves scarce. The feds escorted Rachel and Zac to the vehicle that had followed them earlier and ushered them into the back seat. Zac removed the backpack and set it on his lap.

Zac estimated the drive from Brookline to Center Plaza would take twenty minutes. That's how long he had to figure a way out of their predicament. He'd gotten himself caught up in the FBI's dragnet when he aligned himself with Silas. Given his recent transgression on the bridge, he'd have two strikes against him, both with terrorist undertones. But what scared him the most was the possibility of having to provide a more thorough explanation of the contents of his backpack, or worse, having to surrender it to the authorities.

The agents conversed in low tones on the other side of a metal screen that separated the front and back seats, but Zac paid little attention. His mind raced as he watched Rachel, her fear palpable in the confined space. He hatched an idea, but it had logistics problems. The last jump was a one-way journey to the future, which meant the machine was in mid-cycle. Pressing the launch button now would return them to Silas's office without having to enter new coordinates. Not his preferred destination, but certainly better than staying where they were.

About halfway to their destination, Zac caught Rachel's attention with a *follow-my-lead* look. Rachel frowned before giving a quick nod. Zac slid a little closer to the middle of the seat, and Rachel did the same. Hutch turned around, eyed them both through the cage for a moment, then resumed his conversation with the driver.

Roughly two feet separated Zac and Rachel in the back seat, well within the transport radius. However, both agents sat less than four feet away. At that distance, they would accompany Zac and Rachel back to Silas's office. Such a move would hardly constitute an escape and would initiate a line of questioning that Zac was not prepared to answer.

Ironically, the cage that at first represented their loss of freedom, might help them regain it. Zac studied the metal screen and did some quick calculations. He had done some rudimentary testing to determine how certain materials might block the scan waves from the TRD. After lead, steel had the most jamming properties of the few materials he tried. But he only tested solid steel, not a screen.

As Starsky and Hutch continued their conversation, Zac slipped one arm through the straps of the backpack. He flipped up the safety, exposing the launch button. After a *here-we-go* look at Rachel, he reached for the button. Rachel squeezed her eyes shut just before Zac liberated them from their cage.

CHAPTER 50

Zac gained his feet quickly when they landed on the floor in Silas's office. The room appeared empty, and he blew out his breath.

"Are you all right?"

"I think so," Rachel responded in a weak voice.

Zac pulled her to her feet, then wrapped his arms around her. "I'm sorry, but it was the only way out."

She pushed him away. "I think I'm going to throw up."

"Take a deep breath. It'll pass." He led her over to a chair, and she sat.

Zac squeezed the kink in the back of his neck as he watched Rachel recover from the jump, noting that she'd handled it better than he'd handled his maiden voyage. This trip had been more of a teleportation than a journey through time. The return trip coordinates default to present time, as well as the original departure point. Rachel's symptoms may have been less severe for that reason.

"Feeling better yet?"

Rachel nodded.

"We need to get out of here yesterday."

Rachel stood as Zac walked over to Silas's desk.

"What are you doing?"

"Looking for something we can use as a weapon in case we run into those two Rottweilers."

"Unless he's got another gun in there, I don't think it'll help."

Zac had never fired a gun in his life, and he would bet Rachel hadn't either. He checked one more drawer but found nothing more dangerous than a stapler.

"Forget it, Zac. Let's just go."

Zac opened the door a crack and checked the hall. Empty. He looked at Rachel for directions, and she pointed left. At each turn, he glanced her way, hoping she remembered how she'd gotten from the back door to the office. A couple of times she shrugged, and they would guess. One of their guesses led them down a dead end, forcing them to double back like rats in a maze.

They ran down a flight of stairs. Recognition flashed across Rachel's face, and she pointed to a door at the end of a long hallway. Voices escaped from the other side of a partially open door as they crept down the hall. Zac stopped and held up his hand.

"That's how I came in," Rachel whispered.

They needed another way out. Zac had walked in the front door, but wasn't sure he could find it again. Even if he could, Rachel's car was in the back.

Rachel held her hands up with a *what-the-hell-do-we-do-now* look.

Zac motioned for her to follow and turned around. He tried the first door they reached. The latch clicked softly, and he pushed it open. They scrambled into a storage room. Natural light illuminated the room from two windows. Zac peeked through the blind on the first window. A small, empty parking lot. He motioned for Rachel to take a look.

She peered through the blind, then turned to Zac with a nod.

"Where's your car?" he whispered.

She pointed left. "Around the corner. By the back door."

"How far from the door?"

"I don't know. Maybe fifty feet."

Zac raised the blind slowly. He checked around the window frame for electronic sensors, then pushed the pane up, reasonably sure that opening the window would not set off an alarm. The silence continued unbroken, and he let out his breath. He helped Rachel through the open window, then climbed out himself.

Outside, they hugged the wall, moving toward the back of the building. A glance around the corner revealed Rachel's car where she said it would be. A security camera above the door gave him pause. He hoped its field of vision did not extend too far beyond the entrance. They would cut a wide berth to avoid being seen.

"We need to make a run for the car. You got the keys, right?"

Rachel held them up.

They took off running at full speed. Zac slowed halfway to the car when he noticed it sat on four flat tires.

They stopped on either side of the car.

"Rachel. They slashed the tires."

She glanced down, then back to Zac. "What do we do?"

Before he answered, the back door to the house swung open and Rocco and his doppelgänger charged at them.

"Get inside and lock the door," Zac yelled.

From the passenger seat, Zac entered the coordinates for his apartment into the TRD.

"What are you doing?"

"Getting us out of here."

He worked as the twin terrors continued their charge.

"Hurry!" Rachel shouted, her eyes on the rearview mirror.

Zac finished and a red light flashed as the TRD processed the coordinates and prepared for launch.

"It takes a minute to—"

"We don't have a minute!"

Rocco reached the car and started pounding on Zac's window. Zac held up his arm and placed his finger above the launch button. Rocco's face turned white, and he took a couple of steps back. His partner had no similar experience and pounded harder on Rachel's window.

"What are we waiting for?" Rachel shouted, her voice a full octave higher than normal.

Zac pushed the backpack to the floor and squeezed it between his legs, hoping to put as much steel as possible between the TRD and the goons outside.

The light turned green as Rachel's window shattered.

"Grab my arm," Zac yelled.

Too late. The goon reached in and wrapped a meaty hand around Rachel's wrist.

Zac stopped just before the three of them would have traveled to his living room. He watched helplessly as Rachel struggled to free herself.

Rachel leaned into her attacker and sunk her teeth into his hand. He yelped in pain and released her wrist. Rachel lunged toward Zac and wrapped her arms around his neck.

"Hit it!"

Zac stabbed the button.

CHAPTER 51

Z ac sat on the floor in his living room, TRD between his legs and Rachel hanging from his neck.

"We're safe now," he whispered.

Rachel squeezed tighter.

"It's okay. We're alone in my apartment. Nobody is going to hurt you here."

Rachel slowly released her grip. She looked at Zac, her eyes still clouded in fear. Zac picked up the TRD and led Rachel to the sofa. He sat her down and knelt on the floor in front of her.

"I know you're scared, so am I, but we need a plan. So, let's just breathe. I'll get you a glass of water, then we can talk about what to do next."

Rachel nodded.

Charlie barked from the bedroom, and Zac let him out. He ran to the sofa and jumped into Rachel's lap. After a tearful reunion, Zac handed her a glass of water and sat beside her.

"This whole thing has gotten out of hand, and it's my fault," he said.

"It's not your fault that Silas is a—"

"I nearly got you killed. I can't keep putting you in harm's way."

"We're in this together now."

Zac stood and walked to the window. He pulled the curtain back a couple of inches to see Starsky and Hutch parked a few doors down the street. He let the curtain fall back into place. They watched his apartment, probably waiting for him to return. There's no way they could know he was already inside.

"I'm afraid we need to leave town," he said as he walked back to the sofa.

"Where would we go?"

"I don't know, but we can't stay here."

"Is someone outside?"

Zac hesitated. "FBI."

"Maybe we should just talk to them. They're supposed to be the good guys."

"We just vanished from the back seat of their moving vehicle. Don't you think they're going to want to know how?"

She shrugged.

"And what do you think they're going to do when they find out about that?" He pointed at the TRD.

Another shrug.

"They're going to confiscate it. That's what they're going to do. They'll want to know the truth about what it is." He shook his head slowly. "I can't trust anybody. Not even the good guys."

"Destroy it. You proved it works. Isn't that why you did all this?"

Instead of answering, he stood and walked toward the window again.

"You did it for her. You loved her, and it was a terrible loss. I get that, but you have to stop trying to change history." She sighed. "You need to stop looking for love in the same place you lost it."

He didn't want to admit it, but she was right. He turned and studied her. Lightning had struck twice. At the time, there was nothing he could have done to save Harper, but by some strange, wonderful twist of fate, he'd found Rachel.

She watched him, waiting for his response.

He didn't want to lose her. Not now, not ever. "You're right, and I'm sorry, but right now, we need a plan."

"Silas can't hurt us," she said.

"Not for another three months."

"Then what's your hurry?"

"His boys, Rock 'em and Sock 'em, aren't too happy with me right now. They strike me as stupid enough to take matters into their own hands." He stood by the window and peeked outside. "I don't plan to wait around to see what that looks like."

"We can't stay here," he continued. "They know where I live."

"We could go to my place."

"By now, the FBI is watching your place, too."

Zac's phone rang, and he pulled it from his pocket. He sent the call to voicemail. "Not now, Myles."

"I have an idea," he said as he pulled the TRD from his backpack. "We can hide out at Uncle Fred's until we figure this out."

"We're going there now?"

"As soon as I program this thing." Zac stopped what he was doing. "Hold on. I'll be right back." He walked through the kitchen and into the bedroom.

"What are you doing?"

He returned thirty seconds later and dropped a large duffel bag on the floor.

"What's that?"

"A go bag."

"Are you some kind of spy?"

"No. The TRD could be dangerous in the wrong hands. I figured there might be a time when I'd have to leave town in a hurry." Zac turned his attention back to the TRD, clearing the incomplete cycle from their last trip. He wouldn't make that mistake twice.

"What's in it?"

"Everything I ever put down on paper while I was working on the TRD, some clothes, a couple of burner phones, and the rest of the money from Silas."

Rachel thought about the box of papers she'd given Myles but said nothing.

Charlie jumped down from his perch on the sofa next to Rachel. He ran to the front door and began a series of low growling sounds.

She stood. "What is it, Charlie?"

Zac looked out the window while Rachel followed Charlie. Rocco walked up the steps, reaching for his gun. Zac glanced at the FBI vehicle but detected no movement. Fear robbed him of his voice.

Rachel stopped in front of the door near Charlie. Charlie barked. "What's—"

Before she could finish, the sound of splintering wood filled the room as fragments of the front door exploded inward.

Rachel recoiled, her eyes wide. Two more shots in rapid succession. Rachel's body convulsed in a deadly dance before dropping to the floor.

Terror turned Zac's legs to granite. Unable to move, he watched Charlie run to her lifeless body as blood pooled on the floor.

CHAPTER 52

How could he have let this happen? Zac hadn't spared her life, only to lose her the same day. He had to do something. If he didn't act quickly, he'd be the next victim. Adrenaline surged. He grabbed the TRD, ran to the bedroom, and wedged the chair under the doorknob.

Zac set the TRD on the bed and typed on the tiny keyboard. The location coordinates were easy. The timing would be more difficult. Unlike traveling back six months or a year, he had no margin for error on this trip. He attempted to reconstruct the last ten minutes of his life. He needed to examine every minute, as painful as that might be. Where had he been? What had he been doing? He did not want to run into his past self, for his sake or Rachel's. The size of the apartment only made matters worse.

More wood splintered outside. Charlie barked insistently until he stopped with a yelp. Zac finished entering his best-guess coordinates and watched the red light flash. The door shuddered on its hinges with a loud thud.

He looked up, then back to the flashing light, pleading under his breath.

Zac shoved the TRD in the backpack and flipped up the safety. He couldn't see the light, but it should be ready any second. It had to be.

Another thud. One of the chair legs buckled. A third hit. The chair twisted like a pretzel. Zac pressed the button. Nothing. Rocco raised his gun, a long silencer at the end of the barrel. Zac rolled off the bed with the backpack, pressing the button again as the big ugly goon squeezed the trigger. Blackness and muffled noise, like a gunshot underwater.

Zac found himself on the floor beside the bed when the lights came back on. No pain other than where his elbow had struck the floor. He sat and made a visual assessment. Everything appeared to be intact. Voices drifted in from the living room.

"I have an idea," he heard himself say. "We can hide out at Uncle Fred's until we figure this out."

"We're going there now?"

Zac exhaled sharply, relieved to hear Rachel's voice again. His timing had been nearly perfect. In thirty seconds, the other Zac will walk through the door looking for the go bag. Zac jumped to his feet, grabbed the go-bag from the back of the closet, and crept out the door. The bedroom and bathroom doors opened into the kitchen, outside the line of sight from the living room. He moved like a cat, holding his breath until he'd reached the safety of the bathroom. He left the door open a crack and waited.

When the other Zac entered the bedroom, he rushed out of the bathroom and pulled the bedroom door closed. He locked it from the outside, grateful that he'd never fixed the backward knobs.

Zac rushed into the living room, dropped the bag, and threw his arms around Rachel. He squeezed hard, hoping to keep his tears at bay.

She pushed him back. "You're hurting me."

Zac smiled, unable to hide his relief at seeing her alive.

"What's gotten into you?" She studied him with a confused expression.

"I... it's nothing. I'm sorry." He couldn't bring himself to explain the gory details of the last ten minutes unless absolutely necessary.

"Don't be sorry, just tell me what the hell's going on. You're freaking me out."

"Hey, Rachel," the other Zac called from the bedroom. "Not funny. Let me out."

A wave of terror splashed across Rachel's face. "What was that?"

Zac ignored her and reset the TRD from the last trip.

"How did you do that?" She glanced at Zac and started toward the bedroom.

Zac yelled. "Rachel."

She jumped.

"Get Charlie and sit on the sofa."

Instead of moving, she put her hands on her hips. "Excuse me?"

More noise from the bedroom.

"What's going on?" Rachel glanced in the direction of the bedroom, then back to Zac. Her expression changed from confusion to fear.

He raised his voice again. "Do it NOW."

Rachel recoiled. She scooped up Charlie and sat on the sofa.

"Zac, please tell me what's going on."

Zac continued to program the TRD. "Something bad is going to happen in about three minutes if I don't get this ready to launch." He turned to her. "Promise me you won't let go of Charlie no matter how hard he struggles. And whatever you do, don't go near the front door."

He turned back to the TRD.

Fists landed on the bedroom door. "Dammit, Rachel. What the hell is going on? We don't have time for this. We need to get out of here."

Rachel stood.

"Sit," Zac said without looking up.

"I have to get something from the kitchen."

Zac didn't have the time to stop her. "Don't go near the bedroom."

No reply.

She took too long. "Rachel?"

His words echoed from inside the bedroom.

Zac exhaled. "Ten minutes ago, our friend Rocco shot three bullets through the front door that ended up in your chest."

Rachel returned with the duffel she'd brought when she delivered Charlie. "What?"

"It's true. I jumped back in time to save you. So, please let me do that."

"Who's in the bedroom?"

"I am." Zac finished. The red light flashed. He packed everything and slipped the backpack over his shoulders.

Charlie growled and struggled to free himself.

"Hold him."

"I'm scared."

"Just do what I say, and we'll be all right." He wanted to believe that more than anything.

Charlie barked.

The sound of splintering wood filled the room as fragments of the front door exploded inward.

Rachel flinched. Charlie jumped from her lap.

Two more shots in rapid succession shattered a mirror on the opposite wall.

Rachel screamed.

Zac lunged and caught Charlie by the collar. He handed him to a terrified Rachel. "You got him?"

She nodded quickly.

Zac threw the go-bag over his shoulder. He wrapped his arms around Rachel, squeezing Charlie between them. Behind her back, he flipped up the cover and pressed the button.

Darkness seemed to linger more than on other trips. Heat rose from the ground beneath them. Zac opened his eyes to blinding light. He closed them again. Charlie barked.

"Zac, where are we?"

He opened his eyes to find Rachel staring back. He breathed in the salty air and noticed the white sand beneath them.

"I got the idea from you. It's someplace you wanted to go again."

She sat up and looked around. Charlie scampered off in the sand. "You're kidding," she said, turning back to Zac.

He smiled.

"You're *not* kidding." She giggled.

"Welcome to Costa Rica."

CHAPTER 53

I nappropriately dressed and surrounded by two duffel bags, a backpack, and a little dog, they must have looked like a couple of vagabonds who'd spent the night on the beach. Zac didn't care. Rachel was alive, and he could stop looking over his shoulder. No one would find them now.

Rachel took Charlie for a walk along the beach while Zac stayed with all their stuff. He folded his legs in the sand and stared out at the ocean. They needed a place to stay. Money wouldn't be a problem for a little while. The remainder of Silas's signing bonus would allow them to live comfortably for about six months. Did he feel bad about keeping the money? Silas used him. He tried to steal the TRD and nearly killed Rachel. So, no, not even a little.

Rachel returned with Charlie. The smile on her face was worth the shit storm he'd been through in recent days. "Isn't it beautiful here?"

"You were right about that."

She sat in the sand next to him, and they stared at the surf together.

Zac put his arm around her shoulders. "If you listen hard, you can hear the ocean speak."

"What's it saying right now?"

"Nothing I don't already know."

She gave him a sideways glance with raised eyebrows. "What *do* you know?"

"I know there's no one else I'd rather be here with."

"Good answer."

A week later, they moved into a modest little apartment with an ocean view and a mango tree in the back yard. They used one of the burner phones to call home. Zac checked in on Uncle Fred, who'd met a new lady friend in rehab. He couldn't thank Zac enough for helping him turn his life around, and for the six-hundred-dollar check.

Rachel spoke with her parents to assure them she was doing fine, even though she couldn't reveal her present location. Despite their concern over her last call, they seemed relieved to hear her happy again. Rachel promised to check in with them from time to time.

Living in paradise, Zac allowed himself a break from his old reality. They ate exotic fruits and sampled the local cuisine. They learned to cook and frequented the nearby farmers' markets. Rachel helped him loosen his grip on the past. But even as they relaxed in their new home, an elephant often accompanied them. Neither of them had spoken of the reason they'd fled to Costa Rica or the device that brought them there.

While Zac's recurring dream no longer haunted him, another had taken its place. Nameless, faceless demons imposed their will on a helpless population and threw the world into chaos using more and more advanced versions of his discovery. Zac had traded his soul for thirty pieces of silver, and the world paid dearly for his transgression.

Rachel and Zac sat on their patio beneath a backdrop of stars that stretched to the horizon and disappeared into the black waters of the ocean. A fire crackled in their stone fire pit as Zac made a decision. He excused himself and disappeared into the house after the first few sparks had grown into a blaze.

He returned a few minutes later carrying a cardboard box, his backpack slung over one shoulder.

Rachel watched him set the box down on the edge of the pit. "Is that what I think it is?"

Zac nodded. This wouldn't be easy. He'd been putting off the decision for weeks.

An approving smile flashed across Rachel's face.

While he never meant to hurt anyone, he'd unwittingly created a recipe for disaster. Time to man up and do the right thing, even if it meant potentially forfeiting a Nobel Prize.

Fame had a cost. Even in the right hands, his discovery would change the world in unpredictable ways. In the wrong hands, it would destroy it. He looked over at Rachel. The glow from the fire danced in her eyes. He didn't need fame or fortune. He had everything he wanted.

Sure, he'd need to go back to work, but he loved his work. He could get a job at the University, and Rachel could finally pursue the writing career that she dreamed of. She shared the contents of some of the journals she'd kept since she was old enough to put words on paper. No doubt, she would thrive here, as well.

Zac placed handfuls of loose papers on the fire and watched the flames rise and devour them. He tossed a notebook in, then another. Smoke swirled upward into the night sky like a sacrificial offering. He watched, mesmerized, delaying the inevitable. Relief washed the remaining hard lines of fear and anxiety from Rachel's face as she watched him remove the TRD from his backpack and set it atop the inferno.

His own relief was bittersweet. He'd just closed a door, a door into the past that he'd opened out of love. Or was it fear? He let whatever it was consume him to the point of putting himself and others in harm's way. The weight of responsibility was lifted from his shoulders, carried away in the swirling gray smoke. In hindsight, it was a door that should never have been opened.

That door was closed but not locked. He would log in later tonight and permanently delete his cloud account where he'd backed up his work.

Another door had opened with much to look forward to. A door to love and new opportunities, and perhaps a family of his own. He put his arm around Rachel's shoulders. They watched the gray smoke turn black as the circuit boards hissed and popped amid a rainbow of colored flames.

He'd heard it said that some people are part of our history, but not part of our destiny. Harper may have been both. While Rachel is clearly his destiny, Harper had put her in his path. A selfless act, borne out of tragedy, had saved two people. Perhaps that had been Harper's destiny. Who was he to take that from her?

"I'm proud of you," Rachel whispered.

"For what?"

"For realizing that yesterday is not ours to recover... and for being open to what the future brings."

Zac smiled and pulled her closer. "I had some help."

In an office on the third floor of Maclaurin Building 4, Myles Gordon fired up the smartboard. A login screen appeared when he attempted to access the cloud archives. He'd created a second, secret account for just such an occasion. Zac had disappeared again, MIA with the assistant hired to keep track of him. He'd cleaned out his desk and taken all his work with him, or worse, destroyed it. Myles couldn't let the story end that way.

Forty-four pages resided on a secure server somewhere in the cloud. Forty-four pages that might give him the information he needed to replicate Zac's discovery. He pressed the print button, and the laser printer in the corner came to life, spitting out pages one at a time.

While he waited, he logged in from his laptop to see if Zac had stored anything else on the server. Zac was no dummy, with the possible exception of leaving this much work behind, so Myles checked for hidden files and folders. He removed the filter, and a previously hidden folder named *source code* appeared. A sinister smile snaked across his lips when he opened it.

When the last file landed on his hard drive, he released the breath he'd been holding. The laser printer continued to spit out the pages he'd sent there. After the printer motor went silent, he logged out. He shut everything down and left the office with a stack of warm paper in his hands.

In the relative safety of his own office, Myles sat at his desk and flipped through the stack, stopping now and then for closer examination. He'd be rich beyond his wildest dreams when he brought a teleportation device to market. He spread the papers on his desk, attempting to sort them in some fashion to better understand the machine's capabilities and how to go about replicating it.

Myles frowned as he studied three pages in the middle of the mess. He pushed the others aside and picked up all three. He flipped through them, forward and back, then did it again, slower this time. Myles Gordon looked up from the papers in his hand and stared, eyes glazed, at nothing in particular. A spark ignited in his brain. The spark turned into a flame.

"My God! It's a time machine."

Thank you for investing your valuable time in reading my novel. I hope you enjoyed the story. Please visit **www.davi dhomick.com** for more information about me and my books and to sign up for my mailing list using the button at the top of the page. You can write to me through the site if you're so inclined. I'd love to hear from you.

Word of mouth is the most powerful promotion any book can receive. If you enjoyed this book, please tell your friends. A shout-out on your favorite social media sites would be cool, too.

I want you, the reader, to know that your review is very important to me and to others that may be considering buying this book. You can leave an honest review on Amazon. It doesn't have to be long, just a sentence or two. Your comments are greatly appreciated.

Thank you, and I wish you all the best.